"You've got to break an egg to make an omelet," said Doug Selby, D.A. of Madison County, and he only hoped it would be one that old A.B.C. couldn't digest.

Plenty was on the fire, and Selby knew the only way to solve the case and save his reputation was to act faster than he ever had before. . . . That was when he went to call on A.B.C.

Sylvia Martin and Sheriff Rex Brandon do yeoman service as Doug smashes through to bring his most perplexing case to a triumphant conclusion.

THE _D. A._ BREAKS AN EGG

THE
D. A.
BREAKS AN EGG

Erle Stanley Gardner

WILLIAM MORROW & COMPANY

NEW YORK · 1949

FOREWORD

WHILE THE CLOSING CHAPTERS OF THIS BOOK WERE BEING dictated, I was working with Dr. LeMoyne Snyder on the investigation of a real murder fully as mysterious as any I have chronicled in fiction.

Dr. Snyder is the author of *Homicide Investigation*, generally conceded to be one of the most authoritative textbooks in the field of legal medicine. He is both a lawyer and a doctor. During the past four or five years we have been more or less intimately associated in the investigation of four homicides. I have learned to know him both as a friend and a criminologist. An outstanding medicolegal expert, he is a clever lawyer and a skillful physician and surgeon.

In company with Leonarde Keeler, the famous Polygraph expert who has done so much to perfect the so-called lie detector and elevate it to a position where it is now an invaluable tool in the hands of the criminologist, Dr. Snyder worked on the famous German Crown Jewel case. Not only has Dr. Snyder solved many mysteries, but his knowledge of anatomy and bloodstains enabled him to clear up a homicide in which I was interested. This was one of the cases of the "Court of Last Resort" where Raymond Schindler, the great detective, Dr. LeMoyne Snyder, Leonarde Keeler and I have been working in connection with *Argosy* magazine to reexamine cases of penniless men who have been wrongfully convicted of homicide.

It was while I was working on this book that Rabbi Joshua S. Sperka of Detroit appealed to us on behalf of a broken, penniless Jewish prisoner who has now served some seventeen years of a life sentence for murder. Our preliminary investigation indicates that this man may well be innocent, makes it seem almost certain that sinister influences may well have helped bring about his conviction and have since gone to great lengths to keep his case from being investigated.

Since Dr. Snyder is one of the instructors at the seminars of Homicide Investigation which are sponsored by that remarkable character Captain (Mrs.) Frances G. Lee at the Harvard Medical School, and since I was to attend the next seminar, Dr. Snyder and I investigated this strange murder case, and then drove on to Boston together. While we traveled, I dictated the closing chapters of this book.

The more intimately I am associated with Dr. Snyder the more I respect and admire him. I have now attended two seminars at the Harvard Medical School where he was one of the instructors. I have heard him lecture in the classrooms of Michigan State College, and I have worked with him in the field on two homicides and consulted with him on two others.

He is a modest man. His professional cards as a member of the bar contain no reference to the fact that he is also a physician and surgeon. Only those who have made some study of criminology and homicide investigation know the vast scope of Dr. Snyder's textbook. Intended primarily as a book of instruction for police officers and detectives, it has far exceeded that original scope and has become one of the most widely referred to reference books in the field. Only those who have worked with Dr. Snyder know how invaluable is his highly specialized knowledge, his wide experience, his keen observation.

And so I dedicate this mystery of fiction to that expert solver of mysteries in real life, my friend,

DR. LeMOYNE SNYDER

1

P. L. PADEN PAUSED BRIEFLY TO LIGHT A CIGAR, THEN AS though carrying out a carefully rehearsed operation, stalked importantly down the corridor of the Courthouse.

The "P. L." stood for Phillip Lucillius, but his intimate associates insisted they meant "Powerful Lucky"; and Paden took great pains to encourage this nickname. It suited his purpose to encourage a belief that his various successes were the result of pure luck.

A paunchy, powerful man, he had, at the age of fifty-two, amassed a comfortable fortune which had so far served only to whet his financial appetite.

Paden pushed open the door marked DISTRICT AT-TORNEY—ENTRANCE. A secretary glanced up from her desk, smiled impersonally, said, "Good morning."

Without breaking the tempo of his stride, Paden detoured past her desk.

The secretary jumped up, and became momentarily entangled. Before she could extricate herself, Paden had his hand on the doorknob.

"You can't go in there," she said, running toward him. "That's Mr. Selby's private office."

Paden pushed the door open.

Doug Selby, district attorney of Madison County, seated at the big desk with his back to the window,

1

looked up. His secretary said almost hysterically, "He walked right in, Mr. Selby. He . . ."

Selby pushed the papers on which he had been working to one side, took in the situation with a glance, said, "That's all right. He's in here now. . . . You're Mr. Paden, I believe, the new owner of *The Blade*."

"That's right."

"And I take it," Selby added with a smile, "it's part of an apparently studied approach to ignore business courtesies?"

"I don't wait in the outer offices of my employees, if that's what you mean," Paden said. "You're working for me. I'm a taxpayer."

"There are a good many other taxpayers, Mr. Paden."

"I'm a *big* taxpayer and I want to talk."

"Go ahead and talk."

The secretary in the doorway caught Selby's reassuring nod, and withdrew.

Paden settled himself comfortably in a chair, puffed at his cigar, and shrewdly sized up the tall, wavy-haired young man who sat across the desk.

"Selby, this is a political job. What do you know about politics?"

"Not much, I'm afraid."

"That's the way I size you up."

"However," Selby went on, "very fortunately, Mr. Paden, politics, in the accepted sense of the word, seldom enter into elections in Madison County. The voters have a pretty fair idea of the qualifications of the men who are running for office. They elect the ones they think can do the most good. The backbone of this community is agricultural."

"I know, I know," Paden said impatiently. "All that's

2

going to change. Why do you think I bought *The Blade?*"

"Probably because you were interested in publishing a daily newspaper."

"Because I'm interested in making money."

"There's not a *great* deal of money to be made out of publishing a daily newspaper in a relatively small county seat. The owner of your competitive paper, *The Clarion,* has been here for over ten years and while he's done very well, he hasn't acquired any great riches."

Paden smiled. "For a lawyer, Selby, you don't listen very carefully. I said I bought *The Blade* because I wanted to make money. I didn't say I expected to make it out of publishing the paper. . . . A shrewd publisher can make a lot of money. The paper gives him power. Power makes money. Madison City has been small time. It's about to grow up."

Selby fished a crusted brier pipe from his pocket, tamped tobacco in it, said nothing.

"Now, then," Paden went on, "Madison City is growing up. It's attracting attention. There's a new resort hotel going up in the mountains above the city. People who come to a resort hotel want to be amused.

"The syndicate that's putting up that hotel wants to be assured of a co-operative attitude on the part of the county officials.

"*That's* why I bought *The Blade.*"

Selby smiled. "Evidently you believe in the power school of dramatic expression."

"I get what I want, Selby."

"Always?"

"Yes, sooner or later, by one means or another."

"Okay," Selby said, grinning. "Try another."

3

"I don't get you."

"That's the point, you're not going to. You say you get what you want one way or another. This way isn't going to get you anything. Try another way and try it later."

Paden took the cigar out of his mouth, used it to make little jabbing gestures which emphasized his point. "Get this, Selby," he said. "Politics. Good, hard, practical politics have come to Madison County. I'm putting it on the line."

"I gathered that was what you were trying to say," Selby said. "Incidentally, Mr. Paden, *The Blade* has always been opposed to me, personally and officially."

Paden laughed, a harsh, short, contemptuous laugh. "Look," he said. "You've played beanbag in this county. Now you're going in for big-league baseball. You don't know what it means to have a paper against you. Just wait until the next murder case comes along."

"You sound rather ominous," Selby said, smiling.

"You'd better wake up," Paden told him. "Smart money doesn't go around trying to kowtow to a man after he's elected. It buys the fellow first and then gets him elected."

"I've already been elected," Selby pointed out.

Paden got up from his chair. "All right," he said, carelessly flicking ashes from his cigar on the carpet. "You're elected. Try and *stay* elected, Mr. District Attorney. And remember that the next time a really good murder case breaks—one where the public interest is aroused—you'll find out what it really means to have opposition from a newspaper run by a man who knows how to handle public sentiment."

Selby pushed back his chair. "All right," he said, "I've

4

enjoyed the opposition of your paper ever since I entered public life. You've spouted your carefully rehearsed threats. The answer is *NO!* Now get out and stay out."

Paden hesitated, sizing up the young district attorney. "If you wanted to be smart . . ." he began.

"I know," Selby interrupted, "I could be governor. You'd be surprised how many times I've heard that. I don't want to be smart. I prefer to be honest."

He moved toward Paden.

"All right," the publisher said, hastily jerking the door open. "When you change your mind, let me know."

2

DOROTHY CLIFTON, COMING DOWN THE WINDING MOUNTAIN grade in second gear, swung abruptly over to a wide spot on the left-hand side of the road to survey the panorama beneath her.

Behind her, jagged crests of granite seemed to have been pushed upward by creeping fingers of firs which were banked in solid green on the sides of canyons but diminished into triangular patches on the higher levels. Below was the rolling sweep of foothills, then the orderly squares of orange orchards.

Some two thousand feet below, Madison City glistened white in the sunlight. The deep blue of the sky served to emphasize the hard, white edges of the clouds which drifted along so sedately they seemed like animals moving slowly, grazing as they walked.

At the spot where Dorothy Clifton's convertible was parked, the pine trees had given way to thickets of manzanita, buckthorn and greasewood. Lower down, the hills were studded with sagebrush, then below the level of the sage were slopes covered for the most part with the remnants of grass which had sprouted with the winter and spring rains and was now baked a dull brown. These slopes were contoured with the trails made by feeding cattle. The paved road wound in a series of loops and turns down into the valley below.

At this elevation, there was still some tang of mountain freshness in the air, still some faint scent which had oozed from the pine forests above. And the silence of the high places still clung to the hillsides, so that the sound made by the motor of a big truck a thousand feet below came to Dorothy's ears bereft of the snarling grind of straining gears, sounding only as a low drone, as though the truck and trailer might be some huge heavy-laden bumblebee assisting itself up the grade by using its wings.

"Well," Dorothy said to the scenery below, "here we come. Mother-in-law to be, get out your lorgnette and prepare to administer the maternal squelch. Regardless of what Horace says, I know you're not going to like me —which is one hell of an attitude with which to approach an important interview, according to all the books on salesmanship."

Dorothy made certain the road behind was clear, turned her car back to the highway, threw it in second gear, drove rapidly down the steep grade to the outskirts of Madison City.

She looked at her watch as she approached a service station. It was four-fourteen.

Dorothy swung into the service station, said to the attendant, "Fill it up, if you will, please."

Then, as her eye caught the telephone booth, she reached a sudden decision. It would be two hours later in Chicago. She could probably catch Horace with a telephone call. He would think it foolish and extravagant, but Dorothy could be grateful for the fact she was self-supporting, had her own money and, so far at least, could do with it as she pleased.

She entered the telephone booth, put through a

7

person-to-person call to Horace Lennox in Chicago, and some two minutes later was dropping quarters into the coin box, listening to the reverberations of the gong which registered a series of resonant chimes.

Bong . . . Bong . . . Bong . . . Bong . . . Bong. . . .

"There's your party," the long-distance operator said. "Go ahead, please."

"Hello," Dorothy said.

She could hear the eagerness in Horace Lennox's voice.

"Hello, darling. You're at Madison City?"

"Yes."

"Why the pay station? Why aren't you calling from the house?"

"I haven't officially arrived yet. I'm just getting my nerve up."

He laughed, and said, *"Your* nerve. You won't need any. They'll be crazy about you and I do hope you'll like them."

"Oh I will, Horace. I'm just being a goof, and I wanted to hear the sound of your voice."

"But," he said, "you're just a little dubious or you'd have called *after* you'd seen them. Are you afraid you aren't going to like them, Dorothy?"

"Heavens, no."

He said, "Mother's inclined to be a little formal at times. Particularly when she's trying to put her best foot forward, she becomes a grande dame; but you'll love her, and Moana will welcome you with open arms. I've written her so much about you she feels she knows you. Steve is a darned good kid brother. Just let him talk about the junior college football team. I know you'll like them, Dot."

8

"I know, darling. I just wanted verbal reinforcements. How is it back there?"

"Hot."

"How's the office?"

"Pretty good."

"Making dough?"

"Upper brackets."

She laughed, knowing that Horace, as a young lawyer, was struggling along with only an occasional client, but making contacts, playing for the future, unable at present to afford a stenographer.

"How was the trip?" he asked.

"Fine."

"And the car?"

"Running like a top."

"Leave it to me," Horace Lennox said. "Getting married to a secretary who has invested her savings in a brand-new car. Nothing dumb about me."

"I resent that," Dorothy said. "The shrewdness is entirely on my side of the deal. I invested my savings in a nice shiny automobile so I could catch an up-and-coming lawyer. . . . Do you miss me?"

"And how!"

"I won't be away long," she promised. "I'll make the proper obeisance to the family, and then be headed back."

"You be careful about night driving, honey."

"I will," she promised, knowing that once she had started back she'd burn up the roads from before dawn until midnight every day.

The operator said, "Your three minutes are up," and Dorothy said, " 'By, lover," and hung up.

9

From that point on, events seemed to march through Dorothy's consciousness with the sense of unreality which characterizes a dream so unreal that even in sleep one knows it must be a dream.

There was the big old-fashioned house on Chestnut Street, the moment of anxiety while she stood on the porch, which she had seen so often in pictures, the feeling of panic as she pressed her finger against the button on the doorbell and listened to the reverberating chimes.

Then Mrs. Lennox was answering the door in person, greeting her with a cordial clasp of icy fingers and the hard kiss of thin lips. "My dear, I'm *so* glad to see you! You're one of the family, and I know you *so* well, and yet, my dear, this is the first time I've seen you. You're just like your pictures!

"Children! It's Dorothy!"

Mrs. Lennox put a thin arm around Dorothy's waist and led her through the door into the spacious interior of the big frame house.

3

STANDING IN HER BEDROOM, AFTER EVERYONE HAD SAID those first good nights, and with the door safely closed, Dorothy, thinking back over the events of the afternoon, could not help feeling that the whole thing had been symbolized somehow by that first greeting—the cordiality of an icy hand, the kiss of hard, thin lips.

Dinner had been an ordeal of formality, as though the family, while consciously trying to put its best foot forward, made an attempt at polite small talk which sounded strained, coming as it did from a group where the intimacy of family life prevailed.

It was as though some politely decrepit old man had seated himself in front of a mirror, bowed to his reflected image, and from time to time engaged in attempts to interest his mirrored self in comments, lending a polite interest to his statements on current events, laughing with attempted spontaneity at his own labored jokes.

But all the time there had been peering eyes, an unremitting appraisal. Dorothy might have been a butterfly impaled upon the pin of an anxious curiosity. Had Horace chosen someone who would be able to carry on the family traditions? Watch—watch the way she picks up her fork, the way she handles that salad fork. . . . "Yes, indeed, Dorothy, we've heard so much from

Horace—and weren't you terrified, driving alone? But of course you haven't been as sheltered as, say, Moana. . . . You must get Moana to show you her heirlooms. *Do* have some more of the roast."

And so the meal had finally drawn to a close, leaving Dorothy with an impression of Mrs. Lennox which was exactly what she had anticipated. Steve Lennox had possibilities, once he could break away from the cramped environment of that household. Moana was a puzzle to Dorothy, a green-eyed blonde who should have been vivacious and wasn't. She might have been actuated by some inner mechanism which was wound with a key, guaranteeing so many times to lift the spoon or fork, so many cuts with the knife, so many smiles of polite interest.

With the door of her bedroom closed and locked, Dorothy suddenly began to wonder about Horace.

Dorothy Clifton hated artificiality. She loved spontaneity, natural reactions, and originality. Horace had been inducted into the Army at a time when he had been only a little older than Steve was now, and foreign service, the masculine life of the Army, the exacting requirements of aviation, had, or at least should have, torn his roots free from the family soil and enabled him to transplant himself to an environment where his individuality could find some way of expressing itself.

But, after all, Horace had been *raised* in this atmosphere, must have absorbed a large part of it. Dorothy knew now that his fondness for his family was partially a pride in its impregnable respectability. Despite the fact that he himself had warned her that his mother was one who lived in a little world of her own, and insisted that everyone who penetrated into that world should conform to the plan of architecture laid out by its creator, Horace himself must have absorbed a lot of that in his boyhood. Would it crop out when he had a home of his own?

The night was warm and balmy, drenched with moonlight, and, acting on some impulse, and because she felt far too apprehensive to sleep, Dorothy switched out the light and went over to sit by the window.

She was looking down on the driveway, a driveway blocked by her own car, almost directly beneath her window.

Mrs. Lennox had insisted that the car be left there. She had said no one was going out that evening, but on the slender chance that it might become necessary to remove one of the cars in the garage, Dorothy could leave her keys in the car so it could be backed out of the driveway. It was, she had explained, perfectly all right to leave keys in the car. There were never any thefts from Madison City driveways. Of course, a car left uptown might be "borrowed" for a joy ride, but there were no criminals who would steal cars from driveways. Fortunately, Madison City was thoroughly respectable, a nice place to bring up children. Here, houses were homes, not simply parking places. She did *so* wish Horace would have returned to the home town to open his office.

The moon, which was nearing the full, shone down on white stucco houses, turning them into silver, casting inky black shadows along the well-kept lawns. The air was warm but dry and clear. The night seemed romantic, mysterious and hushed.

Abruptly, Dorothy jerked to attention.

The house belowstairs was dark now, but a figure

13

came gliding noiselessly out from the shadows of the house, a figure which seemed to have emerged from the house and which moved directly toward Dorothy's automobile.

For a moment, swift contrition gripped Dorothy Clifton. She knew she shouldn't have left the automobile there in the driveway, despite the fact that Mrs. Lennox had assured her no one would be going out.

Now someone wanted to go out, and her automobile was in the way and would have to be moved.

Dorothy decided she'd run down and move the car herself.

She rose from the chair and at that moment the figure below looked back toward the house, then up at the window of Dorothy's room.

The moonlight which filtered through showed the face as only a white oval, not even blurred features. Dorothy could not even approximate a guess as to who the person was, but there was something about the furtive poise of the figure which caused Dorothy to halt the impulse to run down and back her car out into the street.

Apparently having become satisfied from the dark room that Dorothy was in bed, the figure opened the car door, cautiously slipped in behind the steering wheel, took off the brake and slipped the gearshift into neutral.

The car, due to the slight elevation of the driveway, began inching slowly back, a silent, noiseless, gradually accelerated retreat down the driveway.

Once as the person in the car touched the brake pedal, the driveway became flooded with red from the brake light, but it was only a brief flicker, then the brakes were released, and the car glided back to the street. The driver turned the steering wheel sharply, and then, but not until then, did a pressure on the starter throb the motor into life. The headlights were switched into brilliant streamers.

Dorothy, at first puzzled by the manner in which her car had been eased out of the driveway, suddenly laughed, said aloud to herself, "Don't call the cops, goosie. Someone merely wants to be courteous and keep from disturbing you. It's simply a matter of parking your car at the curb in order to get another car out, and . . ."

But the driver didn't park Dorothy's car at the curb. Instead, the clutch was slipped in and the automobile purred smoothly down the street in the direction of the business district.

Bewildered, puzzled, Dorothy gave frowning consideration to half a dozen possible explanations. In the end she settled herself in a chair by the window to wait and watch.

Perhaps Mrs. Lennox had merely gone out on some hasty errand, perhaps to a drugstore for some headache medicine and, considering Dorothy as one of the family, had not wished to go to all the trouble of backing Dorothy's car into the street, then opening the garage and getting out one of the family cars.

By eleven-thirty, Dorothy decided that she'd go to bed. Even if her car had been stolen she couldn't very well alarm the household now.

And then, just as she had put on her nightgown and was starting for the bed, she saw headlights dance for a moment on the driveway, and heard the purr of the motor.

She stood at the window looking down, saw that the headlights were extinguished as soon as the car had straightened into the driveway. She saw her car crawl up the driveway to the exact spot where she had left it, saw a woman open the door, slip cautiously to the cement, stand for a few moments listening, then, gently easing the door closed, glide back into the shadows of the house.

From below there was not so much as the sound of a closing door, or the tread of a footstep.

The big house was as quiet as the night.

Dorothy stretched out on the bed, tried to sleep, and with each passing minute felt more restless and more uneasy.

She wondered where this woman had taken her car. Had it been merely on a trip to town, or had she gone on some longer jaunt? Dorothy wished she knew.

Then suddenly she realized she had a means of finding out.

Dorothy had kept a log of her trip across the country and one of her reasons for stopping at the gasoline station, and filling the car with gas as she entered Madison City, was so she could tell exactly how much mileage she had been getting to the gallon on the cross-country run. She had started with a full tank and she would finish with a full tank. And so she had a speedometer reading accurate to within approximately one mile.

Impulse got the better of her. She arose, slipped on a housecoat and soft slippers, opened the door, and gently drifted down the wide staircase. A small pencil flashlight in her hand furnished sufficient illumination so that she could see where she was going.

16

In case she should disturb anyone, she could always say that she had forgotten something in the car.

The house had been massively built with the sturdiness of a prewar era, and had settled to a point where there were no creaking boards. Walking down the carpeted treads of the stairway was easy and noiseless. Then Dorothy crossed the hallway, opened the door to the living room, went through that to the library, and opened the library door which gave access to a side portico which opened directly on the driveway. A moment later she was standing beside the open door of her car.

The flashlight illuminated the face of the speedometer.

The car had only been driven four miles since she had taken the speedometer reading at the gasoline station. Dorothy turned the beam of the flashlight to the back of the car.

Reflected light glittered back from some metallic object on the floor.

Dorothy leaned over the back of the seat.

' It was a woman's purse.

Dorothy tucked the purse under her arm. Quietly as a shadow she re-entered the house, and was halfway up the stairs when she heard the first scream.

That first scream was followed by another and then another.

Lights clicked into brilliance on the upper floor. Dorothy could hear the sound of running feet coming toward the stairs. She realized she was trapped. The screams were coming from a room on the ground floor and on the other side of the house from the library and living room. Dorothy knew vaguely that there were two bedrooms on this side of the house, but hardly knew who slept there.

One more scream sounded from the lower floor, then Moana's cry of, "Mother!"

Dorothy saw a shadow looming on the wall of the staircase. She turned toward the screams.

Mrs. Lennox, now on the stairway behind her, called out sharply, "Who's that?"

Dorothy turned to look back over her shoulder.

"Oh, Mrs. Lennox, did you hear the scream I . . . there it is again."

"Yes," Mrs. Lennox said. "Hurry. It's Moana!"

Dorothy ran toward the bedrooms on the west.

Mrs. Lennox, more familiar with the house, rushed past her, clicked on lights, and flung her weight against a door which refused to budge.

"Moana, Moana!" she cried. "Open up! What's the matter?"

A lock clicked.

Moana Lennox, attired in nightgown and slippers, pointed to an open window. "He must have got in that way," she said.

"What is it?" Dorothy asked.

"Someone got in the window! See, the screen's cut."

"Good heavens, child, *look* at your room!" Mrs. Lennox exclaimed.

Moana nodded mutely.

Dorothy, in the doorway, surveyed the room, drawer contents dumped on the floor in a pile, the contents of a jewel case spilled on top of the bureau so that the lights glittered from costume jewelry.

"What happened?" Mrs. Lennox asked.

"A burglar!" Moana gasped. "I woke up—he was in

the room. I screamed. He ran. I locked the door—and kept screaming, I guess."

Lights were now coming on in adjoining houses.

"Tell me, my darling, did he hurt you? Did he . . ."

"He never touched me," Moana said. "He must have heard me move when something aroused me and I wakened. I had been sleeping very soundly and couldn't imagine what had awakened me, but I had the feeling someone was in the room. . . . I had almost convinced myself it was just a dream when I heard him move. He was moving toward my bed. I screamed, and screamed again. He ran out through that door. I jumped up out of bed, ran to the door and bolted it so he couldn't come back. I switched on the light—and then I realized for the first time that I'd been screaming all of that time. I felt like an absolute ninny."

"Well," Mrs. Lennox said, peering out of the window at the lights which had flashed on in the neighboring house, "I guess now we'll have to notify the police. Dorothy, dear, would you mind going to the telephone and calling the police? Ask them to send out a radio car at once. Oh, I see you have a flashlight—*and* your purse."

Dorothy said, lamely, "I heard the scream and . . ."

"You certainly must be a light sleeper," Mrs. Lennox said, with a peculiar gleam back of the granite in her eyes. "You managed to get on a housecoat, slippers, pick up your purse, find a flashlight, and you must have been well ahead of me. I didn't see you in the corridor or on the stairs."

"I came down the stairs just ahead of you."

"Indeed!" Mrs. Lennox said, acidly. "And now will you please notify the police?"

4

DOUG SELBY WAS WAKENED BY THE SOUND OF GENTLE BUT persistent knuckles on the door of his apartment.

"Doug, oh Doug!"

Selby sat up in bed, switched on the light. "Just a moment," he called.

Selby threw a robe around himself, kicked his feet into slippers, went to the door, then paused cautiously. "Who is it?"

"Rex Brandon, Doug," the sheriff said.

Selby unlocked the door and pulled it open, grinning as he said, "Guess I'm getting a little suspicious, what with one thing and another."

"You keep right on being suspicious," Rex Brandon said. "This county is changing a lot, Doug. Police have found a body down in the park. I left word nothing was to be touched, that they were to rope off a place around the body and block the road in both directions. I thought you'd like to go down."

Selby nodded, started dressing.

The sheriff settled himself in a chair, pulled a cloth sack of tobacco from his pocket, and started rolling a cigarette. His face, grizzled by years spent in the saddle during the time he had been a cattleman, was crinkled with lines of character which made little calipers at the corners of his mouth, crow's-feet out from his eyes, giving him an expression of whimsical good nature.

"What is this body?" Selby asked, getting into his clothes. "Is this a murder?"

"Looks like it," Brandon said. "Otherwise, I wouldn't have got you up."

"Where's Otto Larkin, the chief of police?"

"I don't know, probably on the job. He's going to be tickled to death that this case is within the city limits, so he can strut around and be important. However, I left word that nothing was to be touched and I think that the officer was properly impressed by what I said."

"Larkin will probably wait for us," Selby said, lacing his shoes. "He's been co-operating with us—lately."

He finished with his shoes, picked up his hat and a flashlight, said, "Let's go."

They walked down to the big county car. Brandon said apologetically, "I should have taken a look first, Doug, before I got you out of bed. It may not be anything at all, but from the way it was described to me, I thought it was a case we were going to have to work on, and . . ."

"Now don't start explaining or apologizing," Selby said, grinning. "You know darned well, Rex, that when we're working on a case which may develop into a trial, I want to have a look at the evidence while it's on the ground."

"Well, from all I can gather, this is that kind of a case," Brandon said. "Of course, I got the dope over the telephone. Interesting bit of psychology there, Doug. The man who made the discovery was on the city police force. He telephoned in to headquarters and then he telephoned me."

"The officer himself?"

"The officer himself," Brandon said, smiling. "As far as I know, the night deputy on duty up at the Courthouse hasn't heard a word yet from police headquarters."

"Who was it who notified us?" Selby asked.

"Frank Bassett. You remember he worked on that case involving the unidentified corpse in the auto court, and he seems to be a good man. He's more interested in getting cases solved than he is in trying to grab credit, and *that* means a lot."

Selby laughed and said, "It certainly does mean a lot. You don't encounter that attitude very often. I'll bet Larkin will have fits when we show up, and he hasn't as yet given orders to have us notified."

Brandon grinned. "We'll have to protect Bassett, of course," and then swung the car around the corner, slowed down and eased into the graveled driveway of the park, where a sign said, "Orange Park—Madison Agricultural Station—Limit Twenty Miles per Hour."

Headlights reflected from the white-graveled driveway, giving a brilliant illumination. Then the car came to a barrier in the middle of the driveway, indicating that the road was closed to all traffic.

A big, rawboned man in police uniform, moving with the easy grace of an athlete, stepped out of the shadows, recognized the county car, said, "Hello, Sheriff. How are you, Mr. Selby?"

Selby got out and Bassett, moving close to Brandon, said in a low voice, "I haven't told the Chief . . ."

"It's okay, Frank," Brandon said. "We'll protect you."

"The Chief's over there with the body," Bassett said. They started walking across the grass, then paused as a flashlight blazed into their faces for a moment, then was extinguished. A voice said, "Well, well, Sheriff Brandon and Doug Selby!"

There was surprise in the voice.

Brandon said, in his slow, cowboy drawl, "Hello, Larkin. What's the trouble?"

"How did *you* get here?" Larkin demanded, and then added as an afterthought, "so soon."

"Heard the road was blocked, and that you had something down here," Brandon said. "What seems to be the trouble, Larkin?"

Larkin hesitated a moment, as though he would have liked to ask further questions, but could hardly see his way clear to doing so. "Body of a young woman over here," he said. "Evidently a stabbing job. I haven't touched the body. I'm waiting for the coroner, but I've been looking around a bit."

"Okay, let's take a look," Brandon said cheerfully.

"You must have known it was important in order to get Selby up," Larkin said, curiosity in his voice.

"Why, sure," Brandon said. "You weren't trying to keep it a secret, were you, Otto?"

"No, no. I just wondered—how you—how you got here so quick."

"Oh, we're fast workers," Brandon said. "Where is she?"

"Over here."

They followed the path of Otto Larkin's flashlight along the grass, moistened slightly by evening dew, to the place where suddenly, out of the darkness, a huddled shape absorbed the circle of light.

"I'm waiting for Harry Perkins, the coroner," Larkin explained. "But you can see the stab wound in the back

23

there, right between the shoulder blades. It isn't a messy job, but it must have been right clean to the heart, because apparently she died instantly."

Larkin waited for a question, and when there was none, added with considerable self-importance, "Now, the reason I know she died instantly is because of the bloodstain on the *back* of her jacket. You can see that it's just about evenly distributed around the wound. Now, if she'd been standing up for any length of time after she was stabbed, I figure the blood would have dropped down and there would have been stains on the back of her skirt. There aren't any. The stains are all around the blouse and the jacket, and that's all.

"She must have been conscious when she fell, because she flung out her hands in front of her. That's why the left arm is doubled under and her face is lying on the left arm."

"Any tracks?" Brandon asked.

"Well, now," Larkin said, "when you come right down to it you can't find a track. She's out here on the grass where you can't *expect* to find any tracks. Of course, the gravel driveway won't help any, but there's a strip of dirt between the driveway and the lawn and I've looked along there pretty carefully. You can't see a thing."

"What do you suppose she was doing off this far from the driveway?" Brandon asked. "She must be sixty feet from the driveway."

"Well, the way I reconstruct what happened," Larkin said, self-importantly, "is that she was out here on some sort of a necking party, sitting out here with her boy friend, and something happened and he just stabbed her. He was sitting over on the left-hand side, and he

24

reached his right hand around back of her, as though he were just going to put his arm around her, and then suddenly stabbed. That would make the wound come slanting toward the left.

"And then," Brandon said, "she'd have pitched forward on her face. That right?"

"That's right."

"And what about her legs?"

"Well, they would have sort of straightened out."

"In that event," Brandon said, "the skirts would have remained in position as the legs stretched out, and that would give the effect of having the skirts up. This girl is lying with her skirts neatly smoothed out, just as though she'd been walking and had suddenly pitched forward on her face."

"Or," Larkin said, reluctant to give up his theory, "the man could have sort of straightened her out."

"He *could* have," Brandon said dryly.

The sheriff moved his flashlight around in probing scrutiny. His eyes, accustomed to reading trail on the range, took in every minute detail that was left, even to the grass which had been tramped down by Otto Larkin, and was now slowly straightening.

"Someone knelt by the body right there," Brandon said.

"I did that," Larkin admitted. "I just raised the jacket in order to see about the bloodstains. I could do it without disturbing anything."

Brandon nodded. The beam of his flashlight quested out in widening circles. He walked over to inspect the strip of dirt bicycle path which bordered the graveled driveway, then said, "Look here. You can see where an automobile came up off the graveled roadway and cut across this dirt."

"I know," Larkin said hastily. "I noticed that, but it doesn't mean a thing. It's where some car was crowded a little bit on the turn."

"It could be something else," Brandon said.

"Well, anyhow," Larkin pointed out, "it won't help matters, because you can't see the tire tread pattern."

"What makes you think you can't?"

"Well, look," Larkin said, pointing his flashlight straight down on the tracks.

Brandon said, "Let's try another approach, Larkin. Suppose you put out your flashlight and we'll use just one flashlight."

The sheriff knelt on the grass and pointed his flashlight along the ground so that the lighting came almost directly from one side. He slowly raised the flashlight for a couple of feet, then lowered it again, until he found the point where he obtained maximum efficiency.

"Now," he said, "you can see tire treads on all four wheels. That automobile must have made a pretty sharp turn."

"Well," Larkin admitted dubiously, "it *does* show a little something, but not enough to make any identification of tires."

"We'll send our technician down here to make casts of those tracks," Brandon said.

"You won't get a thing," Larkin warned. "Those distinctive marks aren't deep enough."

"Well, we can try anyway," Brandon said.

They slowly walked back to the body, searching for prints in the grass, finding nothing.

Standing once more above the body, looking down at

26

the features that were visible, Brandon said, "She was a mighty good-looking young girl, Doug."

Selby nodded.

The face was that of a young woman, not over twenty-three or twenty-four. She was copper-haired, light-complexioned, trim-figured.

Selby said, "One peculiar thing, Rex."

"What's that?" the sheriff asked.

"We don't see any sign of a purse," Selby pointed out. "Of course she may be lying on it. We can't tell for certain until we move the body, but it doesn't look as though there's any purse here."

"Say, by George, that's right," Otto Larkin said. "Say, by George, that *is* right. It was a purse snatcher who did this!"

They were silent for a few seconds.

"Say," Otto Larkin announced suddenly, "we've got the whole thing now. This girl was walking along here in the park. This bunch of hoodlums came along in the car. . . . No, now wait a minute, it probably was a one-man job. He pulled the car in alongside of her, and tried to get her to go for a ride. She wouldn't do it, but all the time this fellow was sizing her up, and he finally decided he'd snatch the purse. He jumped out and she started to run. She ran across the lawn, and he chased after her, and ordered her to stop. She probably screamed and he stabbed her through the back. Then he grabbed her purse, ran back to the car, and beat it."

"Of course," Brandon pointed out, "a good blow on the back of the head would have accomplished his purpose, and then he wouldn't have faced the gas chamber in case he was arrested."

"Some of these fellows nowadays," Otto Larkin announced, "just don't give a hoot. They're crazy, absolutely nuts. Things didn't use to be that way."

"I know," the sheriff admitted. "Now that we have these new highways, what with all the overcrowding in the city, we're picking up a percentage of the city population."

Larkin said, "If you ask me, he . . . a couple of cars coming."

They walked over as Bassett stopped the cars at the barrier. One contained Harry Perkins, the coroner, the other Sylvia Martin, the trim, energetic reporter for *The Clarion*.

Sylvia gave the officials a friendly smile, then followed the coroner over to the body.

Perkins, a long, lanky individual, eyed the body. "Darned if it ain't a shame. A good-looking girl like that. Anybody have any idea who she was?"

Larkin said, very importantly, "We didn't want to move her to see if there was a purse underneath the body, but that's going to be the significant thing. If the purse is there, we'll probably find out who she is, and if it isn't there, the mere fact that it ain't is a significant clue, a mighty significant clue."

The coroner bent by the body, felt for a pulse, said, "She's dead, all right." He gently inserted his hand under the body, said, "There's no purse here, gentlemen."

Brandon said, "I want her left here long enough for us to get some photographs and then I want to get a cast of some tire marks over there. I'm going to call my office and get my technician down here."

Selby gently turned back the coat worn by the dead

28

girl. "Here's a label," he said. "The Style Shop—Windrift, Montana."

"Nothing to indicate who *she* is, no initials," Larkin said, his voice showing disappointment. "I was hoping . . . I mean I wondered if she wasn't some local girl . . . good family and all that. She's wearing nice clothes."

Sylvia Martin slipped her gloved hand in under Selby's arm, drew him gently off to one side.

"What are they waiting for?"

"A photographer from the sheriff's office."

Sylvia said, "Gosh, Doug, I've got a deadline to meet in just about half an hour."

Selby said, "There's a chance—perhaps one out of fifty that she's a transient who is registered at the hotel and . . ."

"Oh Doug! Couldn't we . . . ?"

"It's just a chance, Sylvia, a long shot."

"Well, why not, Doug? If she's a transient she's a well-dressed transient who'd be traveling first class, and the Madison Hotel is the place she'd probably be staying.

"Oh, Doug, let's."

Selby thought for a moment, then sauntered over to Brandon. "I suppose you want to stay here until your photographer arrives, Rex."

"I think I'd better, Doug."

Selby lowered his voice so that there would be no chance of Larkin overhearing him. "Sylvia and I are going to drive up to the hotel and see if a woman of this description from Windrift, Montana, is registered there."

"Good idea," Brandon said. "They've sent Bassett out to pick up Bob Terry. As soon as he gets here he

29

can take charge. You and Sylvia go on up and I'll join you at the hotel as soon as I can get away from here."

Selby moved back to Sylvia. "Okay, Sylvia, let's try a short cut to find out who she is. We may be lucky."

Sylvia Martin's eager fingers dug into his arm. "Come on, Doug. You can ride with me. Of *course* we'll be lucky."

He patted her shoulder. "I may need a little luck. Paden, the new owner of *The Blade* called on me and told me the next murder case here would wind me up."

She stopped abruptly. "Oh, Doug, I'm afraid of him. He's . . . he's utterly ruthless."

Selby laughed. "Come on, Sylvia. We'll start off by letting *The Clarion* steal a march on him, identify the murdered girl, notify the home town papers, and get a paragraph or two off to the wire services."

5

THE NIGHT CLERK AT THE MADISON HOTEL HAD TURNED down the lights in the lobby so that the single reading lamp behind the desk bathed the hotel switchboard in white light. He had his feet propped up on a stool and was reading a magazine.

Glancing into the dimly lit lobby, and seeing the two figures approaching, he got to his feet, pulled down his vest, and said, "I'm sorry, we're all filled up. If you . . . why it's Miss Martin and Mr. Selby!"

Selby nodded. "We're trying to find out something about a young woman about twenty-two or twenty-three years old. We think she *may* have a room here. She's probably registered from Windrift, Montana. Good-looking, red-haired, nice figure. Know her?"

"Why, yes, we do have a young woman from Windrift. She's Miss Daphne Arcola, in room six hundred and two. I remember her because she checked in not very long after I came on duty at seven o'clock. She's a very beautiful young woman, stunning. I'd never heard of Windrift, and told her so. She explained to me that it's quite a dude ranching center. She answers the description."

"I see," Selby said. "Will you ring her room, please?"

"*Now?*"

"Yes."

"Well, of course, it's pretty late," the clerk said, glancing significantly at the clock. "Of course . . ." He let his voice trail into silence.

Selby held him with insistent eyes and the clerk hastily added, "However, since *you* request it, Mr. Selby . . ."

He moved over to the switchboard, plugged in a line and pressed a key. After several seconds he pressed it again, then held his finger down firmly.

"She doesn't answer, Mr. Selby."

"I think that's our party," Selby said. "Take a passkey and come on up."

"I'm not supposed to leave the switchboard during the time I'm on duty, seven to three. I'm sorry, Mr. Selby. I . . ."

"Then give us the passkey."

The clerk hesitated for a moment, then with a sigh, took a passkey from a nail. "All right, let's go. I'll take a chance."

They rattled upward in the elevator.

The clerk took the precaution of knocking twice on the door of 602. When he received no answer he inserted the passkey, clicked back the spring lock, opened the door a scant two inches, said, "I beg your pardon," then opened it an inch or two more. "This is the management."

He reached in through the open door, groped for the light switch, then clicked it on.

"Well," the clerk said, "there seems to be no one here."

Selby glanced at Sylvia Martin, and pushed past the clerk into the room.

The clerk said, "Of course this is very irregular."

Selby said, "It's quite regular as far as *I'm* concerned. You can leave if you don't want to have any part in it. Come in, Sylvia. I want you to look things over."

The clerk stood for a moment undecided.

Selby said, "We don't need to detain you any longer and you've been away from the switchboard a few minutes as it is. Just go on down and watch the switchboard. If anyone comes in and asks for Miss Arcola, give us a ring."

"Suppose she should come in?"

"I don't think she will. In case she does, ring the phone three times in quick succession. We'll get out within five seconds after we get the signal. Now, if anyone comes in and takes the elevator to this floor, ring twice in quick succession. Do you understand? Twice for any other person, three times if it's Miss Arcola."

"Yes, sir."

"All right. That's all."

The clerk retired and Selby closed the door.

"She seems to have traveled light, Sylvia. There's only one small suitcase."

"Which hasn't been unpacked."

"She got something out of it, however," Selby said, indicating the oblong pattern on the bedspread. "She put the suitcase on the bed, opened it and took something out, or else put something in."

"Yes, I guess she did. . . . You're right, Doug. She left a pair of stockings and some underthings in the bathroom. I can see them in the washbowl."

"Well," Selby said, grinning, "do your stuff."

Sylvia went over to the suitcase, placed it on a chair and opened it.

"Neatly packed," she observed. "She's evidently done quite a bit of traveling."

"Find anything?" Selby asked.

"Not a thing—dresses, underclothes, stockings, slippers, nightgowns, apparently just the things a girl would need in traveling. Nothing that's personal like papers, letters, diary, anything of that sort."

"There should be an overnight bag somewhere, with lotions and things of that sort, shouldn't there?"

"Uh-huh. There it is over there by the side of the dresser."

"Take a look in that."

"Nothing in here," Sylvia said, after a few moments, "except creams and toilet sundries."

"Take a look at those clothes and see if you can find labels in them, and also take a look for cleaning marks. Leave things just the way they are as nearly as you can, but see if you can't find something which will give us a clue."

Selby walked over to the telephone, picked up the receiver, and after a moment when he heard the clerk's voice on the line, said, "You keep a record of phone calls. Look up this room and see if she made any phone calls."

"Yes, sir. You want to hold the phone?"

"I'll hold it."

"Yes, sir," the man said after an interval. "There are two telephone numbers."

"Local or long-distance?"

"Local."

"What are they?"

"West 9328. That was the first one she called. And then Orange 8967."

34

"Find out the listing on those numbers," Selby said. "I'll hold the line."

"All right, Mr. Selby. Just a minute. . . . Just hold the phone a minute. Someone's coming in. . . . Oh, it's the sheriff. . . . He says to tell you he's coming right on up to the room."

"All right," Selby said. "Get me the listings on those numbers."

Selby held on to the phone while Sylvia finished going through the suitcase.

"I can't find a thing, Doug, that will help. There's a label on a coat from an outfitting company in Los Angeles, and one from a San Francisco department store. She evidently travels and buys clothes here and there as she needs them."

Selby said, "Rex Brandon's on his way up here. He may have some additional information, and . . ."

The clerk said, "I have those numbers for you, Mr. Selby."

"All right, what are they?"

"The West 9328 number is the number of Mrs. Lorraine Lennox at 836 West Chestnut, and the other is that of Mr. Carr."

Selby said, excitedly, "You mean A. B. Carr?"

"That's right, sir. Alfonse Baker Carr, the lawyer."

"When did she call *him?*"

"We don't keep the exact time of the calls. All I can tell is that first she called this number out on Chestnut, and then the Carr number. She arrived here at the hotel about eight o'clock, so it was some time after eight. That's all I can tell. I'm sorry, Mr. Selby, but we just keep those numbers so we can keep our telephone record straight. The time isn't important to us."

"I understand," Selby said.

Rex Brandon opened the door, grinned at Selby, and said, "I see you've struck pay dirt."

"You don't know the half of it," Selby said.

He said to the clerk, "All right, remember the signals. Let me know if anyone asks for this woman and if anyone should telephone and ask for this room, try to find out who's telephoning. Tell them that at this hour of the night you have to keep a record of who's calling. Do you understand that?"

"Yes, sir."

"Okay," Selby said, and hung up the phone. He turned to the sheriff.

"Her name's Daphne Arcola, Rex. She comes from Windrift, Montana. She placed two calls, one of them to Mrs. Lennox, at 836 Chestnut, and the other one you'll never guess."

"Who?"

"Old A. B. C.," Selby said.

Brandon's face darkened. "That shyster."

"Not a shyster," Selby said. "A remarkably clever, dangerous attorney who makes his living by . . ."

"By showing crooks how they can get around the law," Brandon interrupted.

Selby grinned. "Well, he's in quite a predicament at the moment, Rex. Because of that last case he handled, he found himself faced with criminal prosecution and disbarment, so he had to marry the one witness who could have testified against him."

"A marriage of *in*convenience," Sylvia Martin said, laughing. "I'd certainly like to look in on their home life."

36

"It probably would be quite enlightening," Selby said.

"He'll wind up by murdering her," Brandon said darkly. "And do it in some slick way so no one can ever pin it on him. I wouldn't want to be in her shoes."

Sylvia said, "I've often wondered how she feels. She was a working girl, suddenly elevated to a position of comparative wealth, and because one phase of the law has never been construed, A. B. Carr doesn't dare to divorce her until after the three-year statute of limitations has expired. Well, I'm going to have to run on and start pounding away at a typewriter in order to make a deadline. Will you let me know if anything turns up?"

Selby nodded.

"How about that call to the Lennox residence?"

Selby looked at his watch, hesitated, then said, "I suppose we can run out there and interview them quicker than we can get action on the telephone, but in a neighborhood like that we should at least announce that we're coming."

He picked up the telephone receiver and said to the clerk at the desk, "I want you to call back that number, West 9328, the one Miss Arcola called earlier in the evening. I'll hold the telephone."

Sylvia Martin moved over to stand near the door, anxiously watching her wrist watch.

Selby waited while he could hear the connection being made, and then the sound of the intermittent, persistent ringing of the telephone at the other end of the line.

Sylvia said, "Doug, be a sport, and get everything you can over the telephone so I can . . ."

The receiver was lifted at the other end of the line and a woman's precise voice said, "Hello. What is it, please?"

"West 9328?"

"Yes."

"This is Douglas Selby, the district attorney. I'm very sorry to bother you at this hour of the night but it's a matter of considerable importance."

"Yes, what is it, please?"

"May I ask to whom I'm speaking?"

"This is Mrs. Lorraine Lennox."

"Oh, yes, Mrs. Lennox, I'm very sorry that I got you up out of bed, and . . ."

"You didn't get me up out of bed, young man. As a law enforcement officer you should know what's been happening here."

"What's been happening?" Selby repeated.

"Exactly."

"Would you mind telling me to what you're referring, Mrs. Lennox?"

"The call that we put in to the police. Someone broke into my daughter's bedroom two hours ago and stole some very valuable jewelry. We none of us feel like going to bed."

Selby glanced toward Sylvia Martin. "You say someone broke into the house?"

"That's right."

"Into your daughter's bedroom and stole some valuable jewelry?"

"Yes."

Sylvia's eyes were dancing with excitement. She tapped her wrist watch and made frantic signals to Selby.

"May I ask if you received a call earlier this evening from a Miss Daphne Arcola?"

"What does that have to do with it?"

"I'm not certain. It *may* have something to do with it."

"Well," Mrs. Lennox said, "I think you officers are going all around the barn to find the door. Personally, I know no Daphne Arcola and have received no call from her."

"It's quite important," Selby said. "Would you mind asking the other members of your family if any of them received such a call? If no one did I'll have to assume the call came in when no one was home."

"Just hold the phone," Mrs. Lennox said. Then after a short interval she said, "Someone has been here all day. I was here myself, and some of the members of the family have been here as well. There is no possibility the telephone could have rung and not been answered. I have asked, and no one here knows a person named Arcola and no call has been received from anyone by that name. Now, what *I* want to know is what you propose to do about the burglary?"

"We're going to investigate it immediately," Selby said. "You've notified the police?"

"Yes. The police have been here. They left about an hour ago. Frankly, I was not at all favorably impressed."

"Well, we'll see what we can do," Selby promised, and hung up.

Sylvia Martin stood in the doorway. Selby said, "Someone was there all evening, all day in fact. She says no one talked with Daphne Arcola and that if the phone had rung someone was there who would have answered it. Either the clerk here is mistaken or some-

39

one out there is lying. They had a burglary two hours ago. City police were there."

"That's great, Doug. I'm on my way. Will you ring me at the paper if anything more happens within the next ten minutes? I'm off!"

She gently closed the door.

"Well," Selby said, "we may as well start looking around. There's no sign of her purse here, Rex, and there's nothing much to give us a clue, just a suitcase full of the things a girl would ordinarily use in making a trip of short duration. I don't think she intended to be away very long."

Rex Brandon prowled around the room.

"I'm indebted to Sylvia for the appraisal," Selby said. "Evidently she arrived shortly before eight o'clock this evening. She came to the hotel, placed her telephone calls, apparently took a bath, and left these stockings and the lingerie to be washed out in the washbowl to-night."

"And then she went out and got herself killed," Brandon said.

"Exactly."

"Well," Brandon said, "I don't think we're going to find out much about who did it until we find out more about *her*—unless, of course, it was some thug who was riding along in an automobile and saw her in the park, but that doesn't seem very logical to me. In the first place, we don't have that type of criminal here in this agricultural community, and in the second place, I don't see why she would have gone to the park."

Selby said, "Well, we . . ."

He broke off suddenly as the telephone rang sharply two times, in quick succession.

"What's that?" Brandon said.

Selby said, "That's a signal the clerk's giving us. I told him to ring three times in case the girl herself should show up, twice if someone came in and took the elevator to this floor. Of course, it may be anyone with a room on this floor."

Brandon nodded.

Selby crossed over to the light switch by the door, clicked off the lights and left the room in darkness.

They heard the elevator door slide open.

Brandon moved up to stand close to Selby in the darkness, then almost imperceptibly inched his way in front of the district attorney.

Steps sounded on the carpeted corridor outside the door, paused in front of the door of 602. Knuckles tapped gently on the panels of the door.

There was a pause during which the two men in the room could hear each other breathing while the person on the other side of the door waited, then tapped again.

Another pause, and then the knob of the door made noise as it was twisted slowly back.

The sheriff's powerful shoulders pushed back, flattening Doug against the wall. He twisted the spring lock, jerked the door open, grabbed the figure which stood in the corridor and pulled it into the room.

Selby clicked the lights on.

It was A. B. Carr, the veteran criminal attorney, who first recovered his poise.

"Well, well, well," he said, "*good* evening, gentlemen."

Brandon said, "What are you doing here?"

Carr's laugh held good-natured assurance. "I think,

gentlemen," he said, "that is a question that *I* should ask *you*."

Selby moved around behind Carr to close the door.

"Go over there and sit down," Brandon said.

Carr, smiling indulgently, as a parent who is humoring the whims of children in some game, moved over to a chair and seated himself.

He was a tall, graceful man with lines of character deeply etched on his face. His hair was gray at the temples and the Hollywood-style sideburns, the keen quizzical eyes, and above all, the man's complete assurance, combined to make an impression which, as Selby had so frequently pointed out to the sheriff, was as carefully planned as the advertising campaigns in national magazines.

Carr settled himself comfortably in the chair, crossed his legs, selected a cigar from a leather cigar case, carefully placed it in his mouth, scraped a match into flame on the sole of his shoe and said nothing until he had the cigar going in just the way he wanted.

So naturally did the man act, so perfect was the timing of his motions, that he did not give the appearance of one who is trying to get time to think, but rather created the impression of a man who is relaxing among friends, who enjoys the good things of life, and who would therefore make something of a ceremony out of lighting a good cigar.

"I'm afraid, my dear Sheriff," he said, "that you are given to impetuous and thoughtless action. You should have opened the door and invited me in. That business of jumping out at me and grabbing me is rather individualized and unconventional. And it might be dangerous.

"Now, Major Selby, who is learned in the law, will tell you that . . ."

"All right," Selby interrupted, smiling, "suppose we discuss the legal aspects of the situation some other time, Carr. The question is what you're doing here now."

Carr smiled at Selby, puffed on the cigar, said, "Yes, Major, I see your point."

His voice had the resonance of an actor who had made a life-long study of elocution and there was that about the man which compelled attention. As Selby had at one time remarked, "Carr can take five minutes to pick up a law book, find his place in it and start to read, and the jurors will hang onto his every motion with breathless attention. He has the knack of making everything he does seem utterly absorbing."

"As a matter of fact," Carr went on, "I don't have to explain my actions to you gentlemen unless those actions are connected in some way with a crime."

"What makes you think they aren't?" Selby asked.

Carr smiled. "Come, come, Major. You know there hasn't been . . . and yet I wonder why you're here."

Carr's face showed either a momentary flash of worry or else a perfectly simulated flicker of apprehension.

Brandon moved threateningly toward the lawyer. "That's always the way," he said. "We catch you red-handed in something and you try to put *us* on the defensive. Now you tell us what you're doing here and start talking fast—and it had better be good."

"Or else?" Carr asked, flicking ashes from the tip of his cigar with a little finger.

"Or else," Brandon said, "you'll finish that cigar with handcuffs on . . ."

"Tut tut, Sheriff. Would you want to lay yourself open to a suit for false imprisonment?"

"With you I would," Brandon said. "Sue and be damned. And if you think any jury in this community would give you five cents' worth of damage, you don't know the type of people you're dealing with."

Carr stroked the angle of his jaw, then smiled. "You have something there, Sheriff," he said. "You have, for a fact." He made a little bow of surrender, as a sportsman might yield to a victorious antagonist.

But it was to Selby he made his explanation.

Turning his eyes to the district attorney, Carr said, "Frankly, Major, I was paying a social call."

"I'd prefer that you forget the military title," Selby said.

"Ah, yes, I keep forgetting. And yet it really becomes you. I understand you had some distinct success in counterespionage during the war. Your adventures would make interesting . . ."

"We were talking about your visit here," Selby interrupted.

"Yes, yes. Pardon me if I digress, Counselor. Well, as I was saying, this is purely a social visit. The room is occupied by a Miss Daphne Arcola, of Windrift, Montana."

"So we understand," Selby said.

"And, as it happens," Carr said, "she is a friend of my wife."

There was a moment of significant silence.

"Your *wife!*" Brandon exclaimed.

Carr's eyes were cold as he sized the sheriff up. "My wife," he repeated. "Mrs. Alfonse Baker Carr."

"Whom you married," Brandon said, hotly, "so

44

that . . ." He stopped as he felt Selby's fingers digging into his arm.

"Yes?" Carr prompted.

The sheriff remained silent.

"Whom I married legally," Carr said. "She is my wife, Sheriff, and as such entitled to respect. Kindly remember that."

"I'll remember a lot of things," Brandon told him.

"That, of course, is your privilege, Sheriff. And now, gentlemen, I take it that I have explained the purpose of my visit, and in view of the circumstances, I think I'm entitled to an explanation of your visit."

"Do you know this Daphne Arcola by sight?" Selby asked.

"No. She's my wife's friend. I've never seen her."

"Did she know you were coming here?"

"I'm sure I can't say."

"It's late for a social call."

"That's largely relative. We're night owls at our house."

Selby said, "The police found the body of a young woman in the park. She had been stabbed. We have reason to believe the body is that of the woman who rented this room."

Carr's face hardened. "Stabbed?"

"Yes."

"That, gentlemen, is a shame, a damned shame."

"Naturally," Selby said, "we want to apprehend the murderer."

"So I gather."

"Under the circumstances, we are naturally interested in finding out everything we can about this young woman's background."

45

"Indeed yes," Carr said, gravely.

"Therefore . . ." Selby said, and paused significantly.

"As I have explained to you," Carr said, "the young woman is, or was, the friend of Mrs. Carr."

"Has your wife known Miss Arcola for a long time?" Selby asked.

Carr turned to Selby. This time there was no mistaking the twinkle in his eyes. "Frankly, Counselor, I don't know. I have never asked her about her past connections. As you may have gathered, gentlemen, I don't believe in long courtships."

The ghost of a smile twisted the corners of Carr's mouth.

"And how did you happen to come here?" Selby asked.

"Miss Arcola telephoned and left word for Mrs. Carr, who was out at the time, that she was in town and was staying here at the Madison Hotel in Room 602."

"And so *you* came up here?"

"I had other business uptown. Mrs. Carr suggested that I run up here when I had finished."

"At this hour?"

Carr stroked the angle of his chin. "As I've explained, we're night owls at our place. However, the business took longer than I had anticipated."

Selby said affably, "Well, if you are night owls, it probably won't inconvenience Mrs. Carr if we drive out there right now and talk to her."

Carr got to his feet. "She'll be only too glad to have you, gentlemen. Also, I have a recipe for a very delicious hot buttered rum, something extra special, and I happen to have some seventy-year-old rum. I'll be glad to welcome you."

Carr got up and started for the door.

"Just a minute," Brandon said. "We can all go out there together."

Carr showed surprise. "My *dear* Sheriff," he said.

"And in that way," Brandon blurted, "you won't have a chance to coach your wife on what to say."

Carr's face darkened. "Sheriff," he said, ominously, "you insist upon treating me as a criminal. I was perfectly willing to drive out there with you, but I want you to understand I am under no compulsion to do so, and you have no right to order my affairs. I'll go and come as I damn please until such time as I am placed under formal arrest upon some definite charge. I have my own car here, and I intend to drive it home.

"Unfortunately, your official duties apparently necessitate a visit to my house. May I suggest, gentlemen, that you'll be more efficient if you try to be affable, and that it will be much easier for me to extend a reasonable hospitality if you treat me as a citizen and not as a criminal?"

Brandon, on his feet, said, "I *could* send for your wife to come to my office for questioning."

"You could indeed," Carr said, "and she would be only too glad to come, sometime after nine o'clock in the morning. Is that the way you'd like to have it, Sheriff?"

"We'll go out to your house, Carr," Selby said. "It'll be a pleasure to sample your hot buttered rum."

"Thank you, Major," Carr said, bowing. "We'll be glad to have you." And then, turning to the sheriff, he added, significantly, "Both of you."

And Carr strode out through the door of the hotel room into the corridor.

He managed to invest his departure with such an air of dignity that it seemed he was an important personage who had very graciously consented to grant an audience, rather than a person who was about to be interrogated concerning a murder case by the sheriff and district attorney of the county.

Selby grinned, as the door closed, and said, "You have to hand it to him, Rex."

"I'll hand it to him with a bunch of fives one of these days."

Selby shook his head. "The man is clever, Rex. I was particularly amused at his comment that he didn't believe in long courtships."

"I'll say he didn't," Brandon said. "And that little tramp he married is sitting pretty!"

Selby nodded, said, "Don't be too certain she was a tramp, Rex. She knew her way around, but she's a clever girl, with a lot of individuality."

"I'm sorry I said that," Brandon admitted. "I'm mad. A. B. Carr always gets my goat. Let's get out of here, Doug. With the county car, and using the siren, we can still beat him out to his home, and get to talk with his wife before he's had a chance to coach her."

"Well," Selby said, dubiously, "we can *try*, but I'm afraid that's all the good it's going to do us. Carr is clever."

"*He* may be clever," Brandon said, "but *we've* got the siren. Come on."

They waited a few seconds for the elevator, paused briefly in the lobby to instruct the clerk to say nothing to anyone about their search, then sprinted for the big county car which was parked in front of a fireplug fifty feet from the hotel.

Brandon, behind the wheel, gunned the motor, tore out from the curb, gathered speed as he shot down Main Street, past the siren-stopped traffic, and turned up Orange Grove Drive with a scream of protesting tires. A triumphant grin was on his face as he said, "We'll see whether he has the guts to try to race us."

Selby looked back for pursuing headlights. "There doesn't seem to be anything behind us, Rex."

"Damn him, he's ahead of us," Brandon said, and concentrated his attention on piloting the machine up the grade to the exclusive residential district. The city lights began to appear below in twinkling clusters as the county car, roaring around the curves, climbed to a point where each bend in the road opened up a new vista of the slumbering city below.

Brandon muttered triumphantly as he finally slammed the car to a stop in front of Carr's house, "By George, Doug, we beat him to it. He *wasn't* ahead of us!"

Selby said, "He knew he couldn't beat us home, Rex, so he simply stopped at the nearest telephone, coached his wife on what to say, and now he'll come following along in a leisurely manner and apparently be very much surprised to find us here so soon."

Brandon scowled, then suddenly burst out laughing. "Of course that's what he did! Why didn't I realize that was what he'd do? There's something about that fellow that makes me so darned mad I forget to think!"

"Let's wait out here for him," Selby said. "He won't be expecting that."

They switched out the lights in the county car.

49

Brandon spilled tobacco into brown rice paper, rolled it into a cigarette by sheer sense of touch, then scraped a match into flame. So deft was he in his motions that he was smoking before Selby had finished tamping tobacco into his fragrant brier pipe.

They waited for some five minutes. Then headlights swung around a curve, danced for a moment along houses on the other side of the street, then swung back and sent lights stabbing through the rear window of the county car.

A. B. Carr pulled to a stop directly behind them.

Brandon and Doug Selby emerged from the county car.

"Well, well, well," Carr said, with every evidence of surprise. "You beat me here. I thought you'd have gone on in and started questioning, so I didn't hurry. Had a little trouble starting my car."

Selby said, "It's nice up here. We were talking."

"But why didn't you go in? Mrs. Carr would have been only too glad to see you. She knows you, you remember."

And this time there could be no mistaking the significance of Carr's smile.

"Yes," Brandon said dryly, "I remember her quite well. I remember the first time I met her."

Carr led the way up the walk, opened the screen door, then flung open the front door, said, "Hello, dear. We have visitors."

His wife scorned the patent subterfuge of surprise. She came toward them without bothering to remark on the unexpected nature of the visit or the lateness of the hour. She merely gave her hand to Brandon, said, "How are you, Sheriff. It's nice to see you again." Then she placed her hand in Selby's and smiled up at him with impudent eyes. "So nice to see *you* again, Mr. District Attorney. I was wondering if you folks were ever going to pay a social call. You see I owe a great deal to you."

"A very great deal, my dear," Carr said dryly.

"Do come in and be seated. Alfonse, how about one of those hot buttered rums you've been making at night?"

"By a peculiar coincidence," Carr said, emphasizing the adjective slightly, "you have hit upon the very thing which I had previously suggested to these gentlemen, one of my hot buttered rum drinks. Is Lefty around, my dear?"

"I don't know," she said. "He may have retired."

Carr ushered his visitors into the living room, picked up a little bell and tinkled it.

Almost instantly the door from a serving pantry opened and a man, who had every appearance of being a broken-down pugilist in an immaculate white serving coat, said out of the side of his mouth, "Did you ring, sir?"

The incongruity of the situation caused Selby to suppress a smile.

Brandon surveyed the battered countenance of the butler with professional interest, taking due note of the thick lips, the cauliflower ears, the flattened nose, and the permanently swollen eyes.

"You might put on some hot water, Lefty," Carr said. "Get out some of that seventy-year-old rum, the brown sugar, the spices and the butter. I'll put the ingredients together."

"Yes, sir," the man said, and turned obediently.

Carr smiled, and said, "A former client of mine. He's very devoted to me, gentlemen, really very devoted."

"Client!" Brandon snorted.

"That's right, Sheriff."

"I suppose he consulted you in connection with some oil-bearing properties and wanted you to handle the leases," Brandon said sarcastically.

Carr threw back his head and laughed. "Now there, Sheriff," he said, "you have me. You really do. I'll have to admit as much. However, to satisfy the curiosity, which I can see is underlying your bit of repartee, I'm quite certain he really didn't commit the murders for which I defended him—and secured his acquittal."

"Indeed," Selby said.

Carr, smiling at the sheriff, waited for just the proper moment, and then added with perfect timing, "Twice! And now, if you will excuse me, gentlemen, I will see about the hot buttered rum."

Carr moved over toward the door, then paused. His wife crossed her knees, lit a cigarette, and surveyed the two county officials with the cautious appraisal of one sizing up an adversary before engaging in a contest.

Brandon blurted, "I hope you don't hold anything against us or . . ."

She smiled. "On the contrary, I feel I owe a lot to you."

Catching Doug Selby's eye, she closed her own right eye in a strictly mischievous wink.

Old A. B. Carr, standing behind her, moved so he could see her face. She turned and met his glance with a look of cherubic innocence.

"Well," Carr said, "I'll repair to the culinary department and see what can be done about that hot buttered rum."

"You'll have to count me out," Brandon said. "I'm on duty investigating a serious crime."

"Come, come, Sheriff. A little hot buttered rum won't hurt you."

"No, I'm sorry."

"How about you, Counselor?" Carr asked Selby.

"Well," Selby acquiesced, "if you'll promise not to load it."

"But of course," Carr said. "A 'loaded' drink is a betrayal of hospitality and a gustatory crime. It takes just a certain proportion of rum, butter, water, sugar and spices to give the perfect drink. To add too much rum is as bad as adding too much sugar. The whole thing is a beautifully proportioned, streamlined . . ."

"Well, give me a small cup," Brandon interrupted. "I'll go so far as to change my mind."

Carr smiled, nodded, turned back to the door of the butler's pantry, then paused to say, "By the way, my dear, I neglected to mention it, but I'd like very much to have you co-operate with Sheriff Brandon and District Attorney Selby. Just tell them anything. Absolutely anything that you know. It's *so* seldom that we can be completely unreserved with these gentlemen, and they're investigating a tragedy involving a friend of yours."

"A friend of mine?"

"That's right."

"Who?"

"Someone who telephoned you tonight and wanted you . . ."

"Not Daphne!"

53

Carr inclined his head. "I'm afraid it's Daphne, my dear, but I'm quite certain that Major Selby would like to conduct the inquiry in his own way."

"But what in the world? Why Daphne didn't know anyone here. She . . ."

"Exactly, my dear," Carr said. "It's a puzzling problem, but if you'll excuse me I'll withdraw so that the officials can question you without being embarrassed by my presence."

And Carr stepped swiftly through the door into the butler's pantry.

"What happened to Daphne?" Mrs. Carr asked.

Selby said, "She seems to have been stabbed, Mrs. Carr."

"And . . . you mean . . . ?"

"Yes, she died almost instantly."

"Where did it happen?"

"In the park. The body was found there and from indications it would seem that the body had not been transported. The crime must have been committed right there."

"But that's absolutely incredible."

"You had known her for a long time?" Selby asked.

"Fairly long. But Mr. Selby, who on earth would have wanted to murder Daphne? Why she . . ."

"That's exactly what we're here to find out," Brandon interrupted.

"I can't help you at all."

"Perhaps you can help us in a preliminary way," Selby said. "Did she come here to see you?"

"I guess so. She must have . . . well, now wait a minute. Now that you ask the question, I . . . I don't think she did."

"She must have had some reason for coming here."

Mrs. Carr nodded dubiously. "Yes, I suppose so."

"Perhaps it would help to find that reason if you'd tell us a little about her background," Selby said.

She said, "I'll be frank with you, Mr. Selby. You're a good scout. Of course you understand that my relationship here is a strange one. While our marriage was sudden, it was . . . . Well, you understand the circumstances."

Selby nodded.

She said, "I wasn't foolish enough to walk into it with my eyes closed. When my husband suggested that we get married in the interests of what I would call self-preservation, and what you would call thwarting justice, I was smart enough to realize that temporarily I had the whip hand. I insisted upon a marriage settlement which would give me *something* of what I wanted. I knew, of course, that my husband intended only to seal my lips for the three years during which the statute of limitations would run, and then he would get a divorce. And I know that he's shrewd enough so that when he wanted to get that divorce he would make it appear that I was absolutely in the wrong, so he could throw me out without a cent.

"I don't know why I'm telling you all this except that—well, you were nice to me and you're a square shooter and I like you. I want to get the cards on the table and help you just as much as I can, but I'm not kidding you about this marriage, and I'm not kidding myself."

"Go ahead," Selby said.

"All right," she said. "You know my background. I

wasn't any gilded lily. I tried to keep my own self-respect, but . . . well, you know."

"Yes, I know," Selby said.

"I tried to use my head. I had a living to make. I wanted some of the good things of life. I tried to get them. A girl needs friends. There are times when she wants the companionship of her own sex, but situated as I was, such friendships are dangerous. However I formed a few."

"Daphne Arcola?" Selby asked.

"She was one."

"What about her background?"

"Naturally," Mrs. Carr said, "under the circumstances I was hardly in a position to select my friends from the social register."

Selby nodded.

She said, "Daphne and I shared an apartment in Windrift, Montana."

"Wasn't that rather an isolated place for you?" Selby asked.

She smiled. "During certain seasons of the year it wasn't at all isolated. Not when I was there. There were two dude ranches a short distance out of Windrift and the place was fairly crawling with Eastern dudes who had money, wanted to wear cowboy clothes, and had roving eyes."

Sheriff Brandon clamped his lips in a straight line of disapproval. Selby nodded encouragingly. "Go ahead."

She said, "You know the way I played the game, Mr. Selby. I met old A. B. Carr when I was helping with entertainment. I . . . I wasn't exactly a *party* girl. I tried to make my living, however, out of men who wanted entertainment—my dinners, some of my clothes—little things. If a man had a business deal he wanted to put across and wanted the right sort of background . . . well, I was that background. And the dude ranches wanted something easy on the eye as local cowgirls."

"And Daphne Arcola?" Selby asked.

She narrowed her eyes and said, "I never asked any questions of Daphne, nor about Daphne."

"She was playing the same general game you were playing?" Selby asked.

"Apparently she was, and yet . . . well, I'll tell you one thing about Daphne. She was the most close-mouthed, secretive person I ever knew in my life. And I'm no party line myself. I realize that when a woman is lonely, sometimes when perhaps she doubts whether she's making the most out of her life and thinks perhaps she should have—or could have—well, perhaps when she wants to reassure herself, she has a great temptation to confide all to some sympathetic woman companion.

"And it's the most deadly, dangerous thing any woman can do. Women are essentially ruthless with each other.

"Of course, it's dangerous to generalize, but basically women can never have the same frank, free friendships that men have. A woman is essentially a trapper. Man may be the one who hunts and pursues, but when it comes to a showdown the woman is the one who traps. . . . What am I saying? I'm . . ."

"No, go ahead," Selby said. "I'm interested."

"Well," she said, "I'll put it this way. Every woman has some definite objective, something she wants for herself. Some women want marriage, some want enough money to have financial security. . . . Perhaps with most of them it's financial security through marriage. . . . Well, Mr. Selby, the point is that I never knew *what* Daphne wanted."

"And you wrote her and asked her to come here and visit you?" Selby said.

"I didn't invite her to come and visit. I wrote her that I had married, and I . . . well, I admitted to *her* that the circumstances surrounding the marriage were a little unusual."

"Reading between the lines of that letter do you suppose that she could have learned the true state of affairs?"

"Not from the letter."

"How did she learn them then?"

"I'm not certain she did."

"But you *think* she did?"

"She may have."

"What makes you think that?"

"Because she came here."

"Can you amplify that statement a little?"

"Well, Daphne was peculiar. She was deep, and as I say, I could never be certain about her. I wrote her the letter telling her about my marriage more so she would *not* come to California and look me up. It wasn't an invitation to visit. It was a warning to stay away."

"Why?"

"I felt certain that . . . well, after all, Mr. Selby, put yourself in my position. I hardly felt I should start inviting my friends to this house. I'm a legal wife. I'm certainly not an intellectual companion.

"I'll tell you something about my husband. They call him old A. B. C. and he's a criminal attorney; but he's a very remarkable man, Mr. Selby. A very, *very* remarkable man. He's always thinking, studying life. He's strong and shrewd and he likes to manipulate things so events happen the way he wants. Don't ever make any mistake about that man, Mr. Selby. He never does *anything* without a reason.

"I don't think he cares much about money, but he loves to feel that he's manipulating people. Life is like a chess game with him and he loves to plan his moves way ahead, trying to figure what the other man will do and then being all prepared with some smart move which will lead to checkmate.

"I expected, of course, that our married life would be something of a cat-and-dog existence, but that's where I was wrong. I have never encountered anyone more considerate, more courteous, more . . . oh, I'm not kidding myself. I don't think the man's falling in love with me, and I know that when the three years are up he'll find some way to frame me so that I'll be kicked out without the faintest chance to nick him for a dime of alimony.

"And I know that what he's doing now is purely selfish, but you have to admit it's smart. He's facing a three-year sentence of matrimony. He wants to make it as easy on himself as possible. And so we play a great game here, Mr. Selby. We are so beautifully, courteously considerate of each other that, well, I don't think any marriage founded on a great romantic love could have the harmony that this one does."

"I see," Selby said, and then added after a moment, "of course, Carr is smart enough to realize that's the only way he could endure. . . . No, I didn't mean that the way it sounded."

She threw back her head and laughed. "Of course you did, Mr. Selby. You meant it *exactly* that way. You have to mean it that way. It's exactly the way I looked at it, but . . . well, what I'm trying to tell you is that I'm hardly in a position to invite any of my friends to this home.

"On the other hand, in breaking with my former contacts I didn't want to offend them. I didn't know but what at the end of three years I might need them again. So I wrote Daphne a letter, telling her about the marriage, giving her something of a background of my husband, and . . . well, I intimated to her that I was being accepted . . . well, not exactly as a social equal; but that while I was living in a big house . . . well, you can see the idea I tried to put across."

"And how long ago did you write that letter?"

"Five or six weeks."

"And Daphne promptly proceeded to come to Madison City?"

"Yes. Not promptly, but she came."

"And telephoned you?"

"Yes."

"And what did she say when she telephoned?"

"She called when I was out and left a message with the butler." And Eleanor Carr smiled as she referred to the butler.

"Lefty?"

"Yes."

"What was the message?"

"She asked Lefty to tell me she was just passing through Madison City and wanted to say hello, but that she wouldn't be able to get out here to see me. . . . I felt she was being tactful and was properly appreciative. Now I'm not so certain."

"But you asked your husband to go to see her at the hotel?"

"Well, no. I told him . . . you see Lefty delivered the message when my husband was here. Alfonse was very nice. He told me to invite her out here.

"I didn't think any more about it, but old A. B. C., bless his heart, felt that I was being self-conscious and reluctant to invite my friends here—and apparently he went to the hotel to invite her out to the house.

"I guess it was too late—then."

Selby and Brandon exchanged glances.

The door from the serving pantry opened and the butler with the cauliflower ears entered, carrying cups and saucers on a lacquered tray. The tingling aroma of hot spiced rum reached their nostrils.

Carr, who had held the door open for the butler, said, "Sorry to keep you waiting, gentlemen, but this is something in the nature of a special ritual. I made yours rather small, Sheriff, but there's a dividend in case you . . ."

"No, thanks," Brandon said. "I'll be quite happy with this."

The butler served them and they raised cups.

"Here's to crime," A. B. Carr said.

"Delicious," Selby exclaimed, tentatively tasting the drink.

Rex Brandon glanced at Carr with sudden respect. "Say, you *do* have something there! Or will have when it cools a bit. It's boiling."

Carr smiled. "I'm certainly glad you're enjoying it.

61

Now how about you, my dear? Have you given these gentlemen all the information they wanted?"

"I've given them all I had."

"That's fine!" Carr exclaimed. "Splendid. Excellent. It's a pleasure to co-operate with you gentlemen, and naturally we're very much concerned about what happened. Could you tell us something of the circumstances?"

"She was stabbed," Brandon said curtly.

"Indeed. Death was instantaneous?"

"Apparently so."

"In the park I believe you said, Sheriff?"

"Yes."

"I suppose," Carr said, casually, "that you learned of her identity from examining her purse. She probably was carrying the hotel key with her."

Brandon looked at Selby.

Selby said, "As a matter of fact, we simply made a check at the hotel from a physical description."

"I take it, then, the hotel key wasn't in her purse?"

Selby smiled. "This certainly is an excellent hot buttered rum. Is the recipe secret?"

"I have no secrets from you tonight," Carr said. "I'll be glad to have my secretary make a copy of the recipe and send it to you, Counselor."

"Thank you," Selby said.

"We were talking about Miss Arcola's death," Carr went on.

"Oh, yes," Selby said, stirring his drink vigorously to cool it off.

"The knife was left in the body?"

"No, it wasn't."

"That makes it a little difficult," Carr said. "And

there was, I take it, no indication as to the identity of the murderer?"

"What leads you to make such a statement?" Selby asked.

"Well," Carr said, affably, "after all, Counselor, it was more of a question than a statement, but it's a natural assumption in view of the fact that you're here. If you had a more live lead, you would be running it down, rather than sitting here sipping my humble hospitality."

"How do you know *this* isn't a live lead?" Brandon growled.

Carr threw back his head and laughed. "That retort was obvious, of course, my dear Sheriff, but nevertheless effective. I *did* somewhat leave myself open there, didn't I? However, I'll gladly answer your question. I know that this is not a live lead because I know that my wife could not possibly have been implicated in the murder."

And Carr smiled affectionately across at her.

Something in his face caused Mrs. Carr to cease smiling. Selby, watching her, felt certain he saw a swift flicker of consternation cross her features.

Carr, obviously enjoying himself, said speculatively, "Now, the park—that's hardly a place where a stranger would go merely for the purpose of taking a walk. It's more a place for a rendezvous—although, of course, she could have been riding in a car and then been killed and thrown out."

He stopped with his head cocked slightly to one side, his eyebrows raised quizzically.

After a moment's silence, he asked, "No comment, gentlemen?"

"No comment," Brandon said gruffly.

"She could hardly have been thrown out of an automobile," Selby said, "not from the position of the body."

"Ah, you interest me."

"I thought I would."

"Could you explain a little more in detail, Counselor?"

Brandon frowned at Selby, but Selby, apparently interested entirely in the hot buttered rum, said, "Evidently she'd been running or walking, and she was stabbed from behind. She'd pitched forward on her face. Of course, that's merely a surmise. There was blood on the back of her dress, but as nearly as we could tell without moving the body, there was none on the front of the dress. Evidently the stab wound was in the back, deep enough to reach the heart, but not one which would go all the way through the body."

"Naturally," Carr said. "A person almost never encounters a stab wound which goes entirely through the body. That would indicate a sword as a weapon rather than a knife, and a sword is an awkward thing to carry, whereas a knife can be carried in a variety of places. . . . Her purse was lying beside the body, or perhaps she had dropped it when she started to run?"

Selby said, "Now that, of course, is a matter of deduction, something I'm not prepared to comment on at the moment."

He finished the last of his drink, glanced meaningly at Brandon, and said, "Rex, we really have to . . ."

Brandon immediately put down his cup. "I'm sorry," he said, "but we do. We have another lead, and people are waiting for us."

"Well, well," A. B. Carr said, "that's fast work. I hate

64

to see you rush off, gentlemen, but—do come again sometime."

"I probably will," Brandon said.

Selby shook hands. "Thanks for a most delightful drink, and I hope we didn't disturb you."

"Oh, not at all."

When they were back in the county car, Doug Selby threw back his head and laughed.

"Now what's so funny?" Brandon asked. "I feel like growling."

Selby said, "I was just appreciating his technique, Rex. You remember what his wife said. He seldom does anything without a carefully thought-out reason."

"I don't get you."

"The hot buttered rum," Selby said. "It was a delightful experience."

"It was a good drink, I'll say that. He knows how to . . ."

"No, no, not the drink," Selby said, "the idea back of it. You perhaps noticed, Rex, that the drink was boiling hot. It had to be cooled off before . . ."

"I'll say it did. I darned near burned the inside of my mouth out."

"Exactly," Selby said. "And you notice that Carr made no attempt to question us until after he had us sitting around with a drink that we couldn't very well leave without being terribly impolite, and which we couldn't drink without scalding our insides.

"Then, having us pinned to the board, so to speak, he proceeded to query us about the facts surrounding the death."

"Darned if he didn't," Brandon admitted.

"And with particular reference to the purse," Selby said.

"You'd almost think he knew something about that purse," Brandon said thoughtfully.

"He's interested in it all right," Selby said. "And did you notice the look of swift consternation on the face of his wife when he made some comment to the effect that he could guarantee she hadn't been mixed up in the murder?"

"Good Lord, you don't think she was, do you?" Brandon asked.

"Certainly not. But for one moment we saw fear penetrate her mind. Carr may not be able to divorce her for three years, but if she were found guilty of murder and executed, Carr would be safely out of his marital predicament."

"Good Lord!" Brandon exclaimed, momentarily taking his eyes from the road, "you don't think Carr has anything like *that* in mind, do you, Doug?"

"*I* don't," Selby said, "but apparently the thought occurred to his wife as an interesting possibility. And by this time she quite probably knows him better than we do."

6

THE COUNTY CAR CAME TO A STOP IN FRONT OF THE BIG, old-fashioned house on Chestnut.

The place was ablaze with light now and as Selby and Brandon walked up the steps to the porch they were held in the illumination of a porch light so brilliant that great swarms of night-flying insects were circling around the shielded globe.

"They certainly believe in *lots* of light," Brandon said, as he pressed the bell button.

Mrs. Lennox opened the door. "Well," she said, "Sheriff Brandon," and then added after a significant moment, "at last."

Brandon smiled. "The city police take care of you all right?"

"I don't know what you mean by taking care of us. They came out here and snooped around and went out with flashlights and looked around the grounds, and then got in their car and drove away. I don't know what they were looking for."

"Didn't you report a burglar?"

"Yes, hours ago."

"Well, that's probably what they were looking for."

"Well, I hope they didn't expect to find him still *here* in the yard, sitting down and waiting under the window. After all, a burglar isn't paid by the taxpayers. He isn't

67

elected to office. He has to get out and rustle, and . . ."

Brandon smiled. "Well, if the burglar isn't here, the place to look for him is somewhere else. Perhaps that's why the police went away."

"Well," she said, "I didn't mean it to sound that way, but my nerves are all upset. . . . Who's that with you? Is that the district attorney?"

"That's right," Selby said. "I'm Doug Selby."

"Well, I'm Mrs. Lennox. Won't you gentlemen come in? I'm sorry if I've been cross and irritable, but I'm naturally as nervous as a frightened cat. Do come right in and sit down. The folks are all in here, right in this room."

She ushered them into the big room, and said, "This is Steve, my son; Moana, my daughter; Dorothy Clifton, my son's fiancée. . . . No, no, not Steve's, my other son, Horace. He's back East.

"Now, the housekeeper was here, but I sent her out. I see no reason for the cook and the housekeeper to be in on this discussion at all. It has a tendency to make for informality and that's bad for discipline. They were asleep and didn't know a thing until they heard Moana screaming. They sleep over the garage."

"Can you tell us just what happened?" Brandon asked Moana.

She said, in a dull voice, as though she had grown tired of repeating the story, "I went to bed. It was a warm night. I left the window open. I wakened, and thought someone was in the room. I had that most peculiar feeling, and then I heard noises."

"What sort of noises?" Brandon asked.

"Noises as though things were being moved around

68

on the top of the dresser, and then I distinctly heard a drawer being pulled open."

"So what did you do?"

"I'm not entirely clear as to just what happened. I seem to have been a little dazed by the fright and the shock."

"Poor child. Of course she was," Mrs. Lennox said. "It's a horrible experience. Good heavens, we might have all been murdered right in our beds."

"Well, as nearly as you can," Brandon said, "tell us what you think you did."

"Well, I think I said something. I think I said, 'Who's there?' or 'Mother, is that you?' or something, and no one said anything but the noise stopped, and everything was tense and ominously silent."

"Then what?"

"Then I could distinctly hear someone breathing. I was absolutely paralyzed. I was so weak with fright that my mouth was dry. I felt weak and numb all over."

"So what did you do?"

"I finally managed to scream. I know that. I could hear screams, but they sounded as though they were coming from someone else. I seemed to have no volition. I screamed, and as soon as I screamed, I knew that was the worst thing I could do, because I was afraid then he'd choke me; but I couldn't help it, I just kept right on screaming. That frightened him. He ran from the room. I locked my door."

"We don't usually have crimes of that type in Madison City," Selby said. "Would you mind showing us the room where it happened?"

She hesitated.

Mrs. Lennox said, "The police went in there and

69

dusted a few things for fingerprints. They didn't find any." Her tone indicated that if the place had been fairly crawling with fingerprints, the police would still have failed to have made any significant discovery.

"Well, we might take a look," Doug Selby said, "just to get familiar with the surroundings."

Mrs. Lennox looked at him curiously. "Isn't it unusual for the district attorney to be around with the sheriff at this hour of the night on a burglary . . ."

"We think it may connect up with something very serious."

"Well, good heavens! Don't you think this is serious?"

"Just what was missing?" Brandon interpolated hastily.

"Some diamond earrings that have been in the family for generations," Mrs. Lennox said. "Moana's great aunt left them to her. There was also a brooch set with rubies and diamonds, and a pendant."

"Can you put a value on the things that are missing?"

"I would say at least two thousand dollars."

"Perhaps a thousand dollars if you had to sell them," Moana said. "They could never be duplicated—not the antique stuff."

"Two thousand, if it's a penny," Mrs. Lennox snapped. "I guess *I* know what those things are worth."

"Well, let's take a look," Selby said.

Mrs. Lennox led them into Moana's bedroom. "This is just the way the poor girl left it," she said. "I suppose we should at least have made the bed, but . . . well, I thought you should see it exactly as it was."

Brandon looked the place over casually at first, then with greater interest.

70

Selby stood by the doorway for a few minutes, then entered the room.

"There's a screen on the window?" Selby asked.

"Yes, you can see where he cut through the screen, so he could reach the catch."

"You didn't hear the sound of the knife cutting through the screen?" Selby asked Moana, who was standing in the doorway as though reluctant to enter the room.

"Of course not," Mrs. Lennox snapped. "Otherwise, she'd have screamed then and he'd have run away. She told you that the man was here at the bureau when she wakened."

Selby said to Moana, "You kept your jewels in this upper right-hand bureau drawer?"

"Yes."

"You didn't keep the drawer locked?"

"No."

"Our servants have always been scrupulously honest. I've never employed anyone who couldn't give the highest references," Mrs. Lennox said.

"And you didn't see any light?" Selby asked. "Just heard the sounds of someone moving around."

"That's right."

Selby glanced at Brandon. "We're investigating another matter, Mrs. Lennox, and we think that perhaps the two crimes may be related. In other words, they might be the work of the same person. Now, do any of you happen to know a Daphne Arcola from Windrift, Montana?"

"That name again," Mrs. Lennox said. "She's a stranger. We've never heard of her. What makes you think we know her?"

"We've traced a telephone call to this number."

"Then there's some mistake. None of us know anyone by that name. Why is she so important?"

"Because she was murdered tonight in the park—stabbed."

"Murder!" Mrs. Lennox exclaimed. "What's the place coming to? A murder and a burglary in one night!"

"She might have used another name," Selby said.

Silence greeted that remark.

"Well," Selby said, "there *may* have been a mistake in the number which was given us."

"I'm certain there must have been, Mr. Selby."

"So we'll leave you and see if we can get a line on the jewelry. Do you suppose you could make rough sketches of the jewelry and send them to the sheriff's office?"

"Of course. Moana is very talented with art work. We'll send you sketches the very first thing in the morning."

"Thank you, and now good night."

"Good *morning*," Mrs. Lennox corrected him.

Outside Brandon turned to Selby. "What do you make of it, Doug?"

"The jewelry?"

"Yes."

"An inside job," Selby said. "Only someone who knew exactly where the stuff was could have worked in the dark."

"Check," Brandon said. "I was tempted to tell them it's an inside job."

"Not just yet," Selby said. "We'll wait awhile."

7

PROMPTLY AT EIGHT O'CLOCK IN THE MORNING THE TELE-
phone rang.

Selby, who had showered and shaved, picked up the
receiver and heard Brandon's voice saying, "You remember Dorothy Clifton who was out at the Lennox's
house?"

"Yes."

"She wants to talk with you. She says it has to be
completely confidential. She phoned me and I told her
I'd slip her in through the back door of the Courthouse
and into your office. She wants to talk with you *alone*."

Selby said, "Okay, I'll be right up."

"She sounds terribly excited and upset," Brandon said.

"I'm on my way, Rex."

Selby dashed out of his apartment, rushed to the
Courthouse, and found Dorothy Clifton sitting on the
edge of a chair in his private office.

"Hello," he said. "You're early. I take it you have
something important to tell us?"

"Mr. Selby, I have a confession to make."

"In connection with that case last night?"

"In a way, yes."

"*You're* the one whom Daphne Arcola called?" he
inquired, and his eyes suddenly became wary and watch-
ful.

73

"No, no. Heavens, no, not that! But I do find myself in possession of the purse which I believe belonged to Miss Arcola."

"Suppose you start at the beginning and tell me just what happened, just how you met Miss Arcola, and . . ."

"I've never met her. I don't know her, Mr. Selby."

"Yet you have her purse?"

"Yes. I found it in my automobile."

"Indeed," Selby said.

"Now, *please* don't misunderstand me, Mr. Selby. Someone took my automobile last night, someone who took it without my permission. I—I don't like to make guesses as to identities. All I know is that I saw a figure. At the time I *thought* it was that of Moana Lennox, but afterwards I realized that it could have been Mrs. Lennox, or it *might* have been one of the servants."

"That's rather indefinite," Selby said.

She hastened to explain. "I was looking down from the window of my bedroom. There was moonlight, but I was looking into shadow. It's rather difficult to make recognition under those circumstances. Remember, I was almost directly above the figure."

"Well, suppose you tell me exactly what happened."

She went over the events of the evening, her voice calm, realizing as she talked that the district attorney was watching her closely, listening to her every word, not only for the purpose of following what she had to say, but searching for weak points, trying to determine whether her story was a complete fabrication. And, as Dorothy Clifton talked, she began to realize how damning her story sounded.

"Well," Selby said, when she had finished, "first, let's

look in the purse and make an inventory of the contents."

She opened the purse.

"You've already gone through it?" Selby asked.

"Yes."

"So your fingerprints would be on the various articles?"

"I'm afraid so, yes. . . . There . . . there's a large sum of money in there. I didn't count it. And there's a driving license and a letter and a telegram."

Selby opened the purse, spread the articles out on his desk. There was a key to Room 602 at the Madison Hotel, a bundle of currency, lipstick, compact, and a letter.

"Did you read this letter?"

"No."

"Take it out of the envelope?"

"No. I just saw that there was an envelope and a letter. Believe me, Mr. Selby, you'll never know the temptation I had to fight—the temptation to simply drop this purse somewhere in the park where it could be found and try and keep myself entirely out of the picture."

The district attorney thought that over, nodded.

She said, "Try to put yourself in my position. The minute I walked into this office I burned my bridges behind me. Now, my whole life's happiness is shattered."

"Is it that bad?"

"Of course it is. Just look at what happens now. I show up with the purse. I get my name in the papers. It makes for notoriety. But, worse than that, it's a notoriety which implicates the Lennox family.

"You have to know something of the Lennox tempera-

75

ment in order to appreciate the position in which that leaves me, and what it will mean. However, I suppose *you're* not interested in my personal problems, but only in the evidence."

"On the contrary," Selby said, "I'm very much interested. Go ahead."

"Well," she said, "whoever it was that took my car last night was careful to be exceedingly surreptitious about it, and probably to lie about the telephone call. Naturally, the members of the family will hang together.

"Let's suppose for the sake of argument it was Moana who went out and borrowed my car. Then I've dragged the Lennox family into the newspapers, and *I* have the purse of the murdered girl. Oh, I'm all washed up no matter how you figure it!"

"Where is your car now?"

"Downstairs."

Selby said, "I'm sorry about this, Miss Clifton, but we're going to have to check the tires and see if the tracks agree with the tracks of an automobile which had been driven onto the walk near where the body was found."

"Very well."

"In fact," Selby went on, "as you yourself suggested, we're going to have to do a lot of checking, and I'm afraid the situation is going to be embarrassing to you."

"Embarrassing is a gross understatement."

"And, of course," Selby went on, watching her closely, "we are faced with the possibility that this nocturnal prowler who borrowed your car may have been Mrs. Lennox herself."

Dorothy said, "Every time *that* thought comes to me I can feel my flesh crawl. Horace's mother!"

Selby picked up the telephone. "Get me the sheriff's office, please." Then, after a moment, he said, "Rex, I'm coming down to your office. Wait for me there, please, and see that no one knows just what we're talking about."

"I'll be in my private office," Brandon said.

Selby hung up, put the things back into the purse, picked up a brief case, dropped the purse in the brief case, and said to Dorothy Clifton, "You wait here, if you will, please, Miss Clifton."

He left the office, walked down the corridor to the sheriff's office, found Brandon in the private office, and said, "Well, Rex, it's a mess. Some member of the Lennox family is mixed up in this thing. We have a darn nice girl in the office who is throwing away her chance at happiness, and no matter how we play things we're going to be in a mess. However, first, let's go through this purse together."

"How did you get it, Doug? Did Dorothy have it?"

Selby nodded, then briefly told the sheriff the story Dorothy had told him.

"There's a letter in here," Selby finished. "I didn't want to read it while I was with her in there because I didn't want her to know what's in it. You'll get a jolt when you look at the return address on the envelope, Rex. It's that letter from Mrs. A. B. Carr!"

Brandon whistled.

They bent over to read the letter, written on perfumed stationery in a large hand:

Daphne darling:
  This letter will probably come as a great surprise to you. I'm married, and, believe it or not, I've married a rich

77

man! I am now Mrs. Alfonse Baker Carr. How does *that* sound to you, dear?

I know that we always used to talk about what we would do if we could ever manage to marry some rich man, but I can tell you, Daphne, that never has there been anything in our wildest dreams which could even approximate the facts connected with *my* marriage. Facts which I'm not at liberty to even discuss—at least in a letter.

My husband is one of the leading criminal attorneys in Southern California. I understand his clients refer to him as "Old A. B. C.," and whenever there is talk about getting caught or, as they call it in crook jargon, "beating the rap," someone will show that he is wise to the ropes by smiling and saying, "It's just as simple as A. B. C."

My husband is tall and handsome, with clean-cut, regular features, high cheekbones, a square jaw, flowing wavy hair that has turned partially white. He wears sideburns, and looks very much like a banker, or a senator, or perhaps it would be better to say some very distinguished actor or diplomat. He is always exceedingly polite and considerate, but I don't think he is in the least in love with me. Yet he has taken me into his palatial home here in Madison City, and the way he treats me, you'd think he married me for love. He treats me like a *lady!*

Perhaps I should explain that "palatial" home. My husband is trying to retire, but his clients won't let him. He no longer handles the ordinary run-of-the-mill practice, but only takes cases which appeal to him, or because of former attachments with some client, or something of that sort. I think he has all the money he wants and I don't think money means anything to him any more, or ever did mean a lot.

He married me because of certain things that I can't discuss, only they weren't what you're probably thinking. I had thought that perhaps he would see that it was made just a legal marriage and let it go at that. However, I *think* he's afraid that I might get a divorce, and if that happened there might be legal complications. So apparently he is determined that I shall have no cause for divorce, and having decided that he's stuck with me for three years, he's going to make the best of it.

Now that doesn't really explain things either. It's one of the most peculiar situations you ever heard of. It would make a movie look tame by comparison. However, darling, I want you to know that I am married and that my address is here in Madison City, and your letters should be rather circumspect because—well, because . . .

I'm sorry that I can't invite you to visit us, not just yet anyway; but you know how it is. However, if you're ever passing through Madison City, or even if you're in Los Angeles, let me know where you are and I'll try and visit you somewhere and we'll talk over old times a little.

This certainly is a strange world!

And if you're ever in real serious trouble remember that —"*It's just as simple as A. B. C.*"

Lovingly yours,
BABE

Brandon cocked a quizzical eyebrow at the district attorney. "Interesting," he said.

"I'll say! Now take a look at the rest of this stuff, Rex. Here's a book of traveler's checks issued in denominations of ten and twenty dollars. Now that's strange."

"Why?" Brandon asked. "That's the way . . ."

"Sure, that's the way most women in her position would travel," Selby said, "but look at the wad of money she has. Something over sixteen hundred dollars in currency, and yet she has this book which now has . . . let's see what was in it when it was issued."

Selby counted through the traveler's checks and the

torn-off stubs, said, "It was originally issued for seven hundred and fifty dollars. The hundred-odd that's been cashed could just about be her . . . . Oh, oh, here's something folded up very tightly. Looks like a telegram."

Selby unfolded the telegram, said, "Get this, Rex," and spread the yellow paper out on the desk.

The telegram, sent three days before, addressed to Daphne Arcola at Windrift, Montana, simply said, UNDER CIRCUMSTANCES WILL BE GLAD TO SEE YOU. SUGGEST YOU COME TO MADISON CITY, REGISTER IN MADISON HOTEL UNDER YOUR OWN NAME, AND THEN CONTACT.

"And the telegram is signed simply 'ALPHABET-ICALLY SIMPLE,' " Brandon said, "and was sent from Los Angeles."

The two men looked at each other.

"Well," Selby said, "we have one trump card *this* time."

"What's that?"

"The man can't commit bigamy," Selby explained, grinning. "He can't marry any more witnesses."

Brandon grinned. "You have something there, Doug."

"Let's go down and look at the tires on that car and see if they check with the impressions we found there in the soil," Selby said.

They walked down the stairs of the Courthouse and then out the back way to the parking lot in the rear which was usually reserved for county cars.

"Take a look for one with an out-of-state license," Selby said. "A . . . here it is, two-door convertible. Let's be a little casual about looking it over, Rex. We don't want to attract a crowd of spectators."

They walked around the car, giving careful attention to the tires.

"Well?" Selby asked.

"It's the one," Brandon said grimly.

"Well, let's keep it to ourselves for the moment, Rex. We'll have to impound the car, of course, but we can do it so it won't attract attention—and I'm going to take that key, go back to Room 602 in the Madison Hotel and search that baggage some more. Now that I know what we're up against, I'm going to feel my way."

"Just what *are* we up against?" Brandon asked.

Selby said simply, "We're up against old A. B. C."

8

SELBY, WALKING DOWN THE SIXTH-FLOOR CORRIDOR OF THE Madison Hotel, took from his pocket the key to Room 602, inserted it in the spring lock, clicked back the bolt, stepped into the hotel room and closed the door behind him.

The room was dark, the windows closed. Only a relatively small amount of diffused daylight filtered through the drawn shades into the room.

Selby noticed at once that there had been several changes in the room since he and Brandon had left it, changes which he presumed were due to an invasion by Otto Larkin, the officious chief of the Madison City police.

The suitcase had been unpacked and the garments spread over the back and across the arms of a chair. Bottles and jars had been placed on the dressing table.

Selby frowned irritably. He had wanted to study the way that suitcase had been packed. He felt that he might get a clue to . . . .

Something sounded unmistakably like the creaking of a bedspring.

Selby whirled, noticing even in the dim light that the bed was no longer neatly smoothed down with the counterpane in place and . . . .

With a quick, explosive motion, the covers were

thrown back. A young woman, clad in sheer gossamer silk, gave Selby a glimpse of long white legs as she flung herself out of bed to the floor, stood for a moment with the silken nightgown falling about her. Suddenly as realization of Selby's presence gripped her, she reached for a robe which was thrown across the bottom of the bed. Then, evidently thinking better of it, she jumped back into the bed and pulled the covers up close to her chin. "What are you doing here?" she demanded angrily. "How *dare* you enter my room!"

Selby stood, wordless in surprise.

"Why you . . . you *thief* . . . you Peeping Tom . . . you . . . !"

"Just a moment," Selby said. "I . . ."

"Yes, you what?"

"I . . . *Who* are you?"

"I *like* that," she said, reaching for the telephone. "I'll show you who I am. I . . ."

"Wait," Selby said. "I'm the district attorney of this county. I'm investigating a murder, and . . ."

"A murder—what *are* you talking about?"

"The occupant of this room," Selby said, "was murdered. The hotel had absolutely no right to rent this room again until it was released by the police. I'm the district attorney of this county, and I . . ."

"Who was murdered?"

"The occupant of the room."

"When?"

"Last night."

"It's news to me," she said. "So you're the district attorney."

"Yes."

"Switch on that light," she said. "Let's have a look at you."

Selby found the light switch, clicked the room into brilliance.

The girl who was seated in the bed had red hair. Her blue eyes had ceased to be startled and showed amused appraisal. Her skin was creamy smooth, and Selby had seen enough of her figure when she had jumped out of bed to realize that she would have passed muster on any bathing beach.

"Well," she said, "they have good-looking district attorneys in this community."

She pushed herself upward in bed, let go her hold on the covers to reach over for the extra pillow and, with a careless, graceful gesture of her arm, swept the pillow behind her head as she propped her back against the head of the bed.

She made no move to retrieve the covers which had furnished a protecting screen.

Instead, she reached casually over to the bedside table, extracted a cigarette from an open pack, tapped it gently on the edge of the table, placed it in her parted lips, snapped a match into flame, lit the cigarette, inhaled deeply, and smiled at Selby's evident uneasiness.

"What's the matter?" she asked. "Don't you know that women smoke when they wake up in the morning?"

"It isn't that."

"Oh I see. You're married and your wife doesn't smoke. You don't approve."

"No," Selby said.

"No what?"

"I'm not married."

84

"Interesting," she murmured. "Tell me about the murder."

"The occupant of this room," Selby said, "left here and went for a walk in our park. Someone slipped up behind her and slipped a dagger into her back, penetrating her heart. Death was instantaneous."

"How long did she have the room?"

"Apparently not very long. She arrived sometime between seven and eight, chatted with the night clerk who's on duty from seven to three, made a couple of telephone calls, bathed, went out and got herself murdered."

"When?" she asked.

"Last night. The hotel had absolutely no right renting this room again. It . . ."

"I rented it last night," she said.

"Well, they had no right to let you have it."

"It was all in order when I moved in. And I rented it at about seven-thirty or eight, and I remember chatting with the clerk on duty."

Selby experienced a sensation of sickening apprehension. "What," he asked, "is your name?"

"Daphne Arcola," she said. "What's yours?"

For a long moment Selby stood silent.

"Well?" she demanded.

"My name," he said, "is Selby. You say that you're Daphne Arcola?"

"Yes."

"Any way of proving it?"

She laughed. "The situation," she said, "is not without its humorous aspect. A man surreptitiously enters my bedroom and then asks me if *I* can prove *my* identity."

"The name of the woman who was murdered was Daphne Arcola," Selby said.

"Say, who are you kidding?"

"No, that's the truth."

"Well," she said, "I'm rather a healthy corpse. Look me over. But, I guess you already have. Say, what sort of a gag is this?"

"Can you prove that you're Daphne Arcola?"

"Of course I can."

"We might start with a driving license," Selby said.

"Oh, I see what you're getting at now."

"What," Selby asked, "am I getting at?"

"My purse was stolen. Apparently you have some way of knowing that."

"When was it stolen?"

"I went to a movie. My purse was on the seat beside me. When I got up to leave the purse wasn't there."

"Did you complain to the management?"

"Don't be silly. The management isn't responsible for purses. I had it coming to me I guess, and I had a lot of money in it, too."

"How much?"

"Oh, a hundred-odd dollars in small stuff, fifteen hundred dollars in big bills, and some traveler's checks."

"And what time did you come in and get to bed?"

"What's the matter, is there a curfew in this town?"

"I want to know."

"Is it any of your business?"

"I think it is."

She said, "You've been asking a lot of questions. Suppose *you* show *me* that *you're* the person you're supposed to be."

Selby took a cardcase from his pocket, moved over to

show her one of his cards as district attorney of Madison County. Then he showed her a driving licinse.

She studied them thoughtfully, said, "Yes, I guess you're okay," and moved her feet over, making a place for him to sit on the foot of the bed. "So I'm supposed to have been murdered," she said.

"What time did you get back to the hotel?" Selby asked, "and *how* did you get in?"

"By asking the clerk who was on duty at the time for the key to this room. It wasn't the one I'd chatted with earlier in the evening."

"Then it must have been later than three in the morning."

She laughed, "What powers of deduction you have, Mr. District Attorney!"

"What time *did* you get in?"

"I'm certain I couldn't say. What time is it now?"

"It's getting along toward ten o'clock."

She said, "That's a mean trick getting a girl up at this hour. I intended to sleep until one or two o'clock."

"You still haven't told me what time you got in."

"Well, it's none of your business."

"I think it is. Not only were you supposed to be murdered, but I haven't convinced myself yet that you're the person you claim to be."

"Oh, come, Mr. Selby. I wasn't that suspicious with *you.*"

"You didn't have to be. I showed you a card and a driving license."

"I'd show you mine if I hadn't lost my purse."

"So that now you're without money?" Selby asked.

"I'm left without money. What's more, I'm left without lipstick. Fortunately I had some extra cigarettes in my suitcase. As a matter of fact, Mr. Selby, I now find myself broke in a cruel world. I don't even have money enough to pay my hotel bill, and I understand that's a crime—beating a hotel bill. Can I count upon your interceding in your official capacity?"

Selby said doggedly, "I want to know what time you got in."

"Well, if it's any of your damn business," she flared, "it was about four-thirty this morning."

"Wasn't that rather late?"

"It depends on what you think. It evidently was pretty late for this hick town."

"And where were you?"

"If you want to know, I met a man. He looked good to me. He had a nice car. We went for a ride. He wanted to show me the lights of the town from up here on the mountain. I presume that's the local equivalent of showing a girl your collection of etchings."

"Do you know who this man was?"

"Not a bad chap," she said. "He said his name was Jim. Anyway, he let me have everything I wanted to drink, including the choice brands of Scotch. He took me where I wanted to go, and he paid the bills."

"Know his last name?"

"I didn't ask him his last name and he didn't ask me mine. When you come right down to it I suppose he's married and has a family, but he was on the loose for an evening, and I was stuck here in this burg and didn't want to go to bed with the chickens, so we stepped out and . . ."

"Could you identify him if you saw him again?"

"Of course I could. I wasn't blind. I'll let a man pick me up once in a while if he appeals to me, but I don't

88

go out with every Tom, Dick, or Harry. In other words, I'm selective."

"Did you say anything to him about losing your purse?"

She laughed, and said, "Don't be silly. Why should I spoil a beautiful evening?"

"You mean casually mentioning that your purse had been stolen would have ruined a beautiful evening?"

She said, "I thought for a while you were going to be different, but I can see you're not. You're just a sweet, unsophisticated lad from a hick town."

"What do you mean by that?"

She said, "Suppose *you'd* picked up a girl right after a movie. You take her out to a couple of night spots. You buy drinks and dance, and begin to look her over carefully, wondering just where she came from, just how sophisticated she is, and just how far she'll go, and then she suddenly tells you that she hasn't a cent in the world; that someone just stole her purse while she was sitting in the movie; that she's lost sixteen hundred bucks in currency and six or seven hundred dollars in traveler's checks. What happens? I'll tell you what happens," she went on, answering her own question. "The guy immediately thinks you're a professional; that you're taking a nice way of putting a price tag on your-self and he starts thinking in terms of cold hard cash, and from there on your evening is ruined any way you've a mind to take it."

"Yes," Selby said thoughtfully, "I can see your point."

"I can get the traveler's checks back," she said. "They'll replace them when I make an affidavit of loss. I won't have to wait too long for that. I suppose the hotel will give me credit until then, under the circumstances—although they may get nasty. I don't suppose I can use *you* as a reference?"

"Reference to what?"

"To the fact that I lost my purse."

"The only way I know you lost your purse," Selby said, "is because you've told me you've lost your purse. Why don't you tell the management of the hotel the same story?"

"I can see the skeptical legal mind at work. I guess you're the district attorney, all right. Oh, well, I've been on my own before. I can take it, I guess."

"So you were out with a man whose name was Jim. You were out until four-thirty this morning. You don't know his last name."

"That's right."

"Nor the license of his car."

"It was a slick convertible. I didn't take the license number. I'm not that kind. Of course, if it had been serious, I'd have found out a little more about him. As it was, it was just an interlude helping pass yesterday into today, and reconciling me to the fact that I'd come to a place where they roll the sidewalks up and put them in mothballs at nine or ten o'clock at night."

"Why did you come here?" Selby asked.

"I came here because I wanted to. I suppose, Mr. Selby, that if I'd really been murdered, that would have given you a legal right to have asked me a lot of questions which, under the circumstances, I wouldn't have been in a position to answer."

She smiled at her own joke.

"And in view of the fact that you haven't been murdered?" Selby said.

"I certainly don't have to let you invade the privacy

of my bedroom to hold me to account for not having been murdered. And now, Mr. Douglas Selby, District Attorney of Madison County, if you'll get the hell out of my bedroom, I feel the urge to take a shower, inasmuch as you have disrupted my night's sleep."

"But I want to know . . ."

"I daresay you do. *I* want to take a shower. I'll see you later."

"Look here," Selby said, "is there anyone in town who can identify you, anyone whom you know?"

"Yes, but I hate to call on her."

"Who?"

"She's a girl I used to know. She's married now. I don't want to bother her."

"What's her name?"

"Her name's Babe, but now she's married to some attorney, a man by the name of . . . Let me see. . . . I can't recall it. I'll have to look it up. Damn it, and that letter was in my purse, the one that was stolen."

"What was her name before she was married?"

"Babe Harlan—that is, we called her Babe, but I guess her real name was Eleanor."

"And you don't know the name of the man she married?"

"Perhaps I can recall it after a while, but I've forgotten it. I don't suppose you'd be a good scout and ask the hotel to okay my charges for a few days until I can make an affidavit on my lost traveler's checks? I guess I'll have breakfast sent up to the room and at least be that much ahead."

Selby said, "Did you receive a wire from . . . ?"

"Mr. Selby, I've told you that I'm going to get up out

of bed and take a shower. I'm going to put on a robe and have breakfast in my room. I . . ."

"I'm interested in knowing whether you came here as a result of a wire you received."

"You say you haven't been married," she said. "In about four seconds you're going to learn a lot about the way a woman performs her toilette, because I'm going to get up and . . ."

"I want to know . . ."

"I presume," she said, "this being a small town, the local inhabitants would be quite scandalized when the waiter who brings up my breakfast finds you sitting here tête-à-tête with a nude woman."

"You're not nude," Selby said.

She flung back the covers. "But I'm going to be."

Selby opened the door and walked out.

Mocking laughter followed him into the corridor.

9

HARRY P. ELROD, REPORTER FOR "THE BLADE," THE EVE-
ning paper which was bitterly hostile to the administra-
tion, was quite evidently enjoying himself. "My new
publisher, Phillip L. Paden, asked me to extend greet-
ings," he said. "I understand he had a nice chat with the
district attorney yesterday."

Sheriff Brandon, unmistakably ill at ease, looked at
his watch, and said, "We haven't all day to sit here and
swap talk with you, Elrod."

Elrod grinned. "That means you have a live clue,
Sheriff? You've already got a live corpse."

"It means I'm busy."

"Too busy to talk with the press."

"We're talking with you, aren't we?"

"Do you mean to imply there's some urgent development that . . ."

"It means we're working on a murder case," Brandon
said, "and while we're willing to play ball with the
press, even a hostile paper represented by a . . ."

Selby interrupted suavely to say, "We'll be glad to
answer any questions we can, Elrod. We have several
leads that we're running down. We can't tell whether
any of them are what you might call hot leads until
after we've investigated them."

Elrod, a slender, sharp-tongued, skeptical bit of news-

93

paper driftwood from the big city, turned his attention to Selby. His eyes sparkled shrewdly as he developed the background of what he knew was going to be the story of the year so far as *The Blade* was concerned.

A shrewd, scheming man of considerable ingenuity, his hard-drinking propensities had caused him to drift from the field of metropolitan journalism into Madison City where he displayed an open contempt for the "hick atmosphere."

That patronizing contempt had alienated people whose friendship a successful county seat reporter should have cultivated, but the man's brilliance, audacity, and facile pen had caused most of the officials to fear his anger or sarcasm. And the net result had been fully as advantageous to Elrod as though he had enjoyed the friendship of those who catered to him through fear.

"It ain't how you get in that counts, it's what you take out" was his favorite expression.

"Well, now, Mr. Selby," he said, "that brings up a very interesting point. *How* did you happen to make this mistake of identifying the corpse as being that of Daphne Arcola, a young woman who insists, in an exclusive interview given to *The Blade* an hour ago, that she is very much alive?"

Elrod grinned gleefully.

"I didn't identify the body," Selby said.

"Didn't you tell the night clerk at the hotel . . ."

"I told the night clerk at the hotel that I was interested in finding out whatever I could about a redheaded woman in her twenties from Windrift, Montana."

"And how did you know she came from Windrift?"

"There was a label in the jacket she was wearing, showing it had been sold in Windrift."

"So you searched Daphne Arcola's room, after first calling in the press—*the competitive press,* Mr. Selby."

"I didn't call in anyone," Selby said. "The representative of *The Clarion* was with me when I went to the hotel. If you had been there, doubtless you would have been accorded the same privileges."

"May I quote you on that?" Elrod asked sarcastically.

"You may quote me on anything I say to you," Selby said. "If I had anything to say that was off the record I'd not trust it to the discretion of *The Blade.* And you can quote me on that, too."

"I'll do so," Elrod said, his pencil flying over the folded sheets of newsprint propped against his knee.

Selby waited for the next question. Brandon eyed the reporter with hostility.

"Now let's see, Mr. District Attorney, you find someone wearing a coat purchased in Windrift, Montana. You immediately grab a representative of the press and go dashing about town for the purpose of breaking into the rooms of anyone you can find who happens to be registered from Windrift, Montana . . ."

"All right," Brandon exploded, getting up out of his chair. "You and your dirty, lying . . ."

"Hold it, Rex," Selby said.

Elrod glanced from one to the other, grinning gleefully. "Go right ahead, gentlemen. Were you planning on assaulting me, Sheriff? By all means finish what you were going to say. I don't want all my quotes to be from the district attorney."

"He was about to tell you that any questions you want to ask of us as public officials, you may ask at this time, but that any criticisms should be saved for publication in your paper," Selby said.

"Well, well," Elrod observed. "How marvelous it is that you can read his mind so easily. *I* had thought he was going to say something entirely different."

"Did you?" Selby asked suavely. "I'm certain he wasn't. You see, I've known Brandon for such a long time I can tell *exactly* what he has in mind."

And Selby's eyes caught and held those of the sheriff, forcing him, by the insistent steady pressure of their concentration, back to his chair.

"You still haven't answered my question," Elrod said, "about barging into rooms simply because the occupant came from Windrift, Montana."

"And answered the description of the woman who had been murdered?"

"Well, that depends on how you phrase the description," Elrod said. "I've seen the body, and I've talked with Daphne Arcola. In fact, I have an *exclusive* interview from her, and . . ." And Elrod broke off to glance gloatingly at the officials.

"Now, then," he went on, "the murdered girl had red hair. She had blue eyes. The resemblance just about ends there. There was a difference in height; there was a difference in weight; there was a difference in age."

"*I* didn't have the two to compare," Selby said.

"Oh, of course, of course. I suppose if you'd been district attorney of Los Angeles and a woman had been killed with the label of a San Francisco department store on her garments, you'd have insisted on searching the rooms of every woman from San Francisco."

"That's not a comparable situation," Selby said, "and you know it."

"No, I suppose not. I'm just trying to get what you consider *is* a comparable situation."

Abruptly, Selby got to his feet, said, "I think we've answered all of your pertinent questions."

"Well, Mr. Selby," Elrod said, "I have been instructed to advise you that the position of *The Blade* is that your actions were exceedingly bucolic."

"*The Blade* may take any position it damn pleases."

Elrod pushed the folded newsprint back into his pocket, shoved the pencil into the side pocket of his coat, grinned maliciously, and walked to the door. "That is another good quote," he called back over his shoulder.

"I think it would be worth what it would cost just to take that guy to pieces," Brandon said.

Selby shook his head, lit his pipe, said, "It isn't the man. It's the paper. And he's caught me off first base, Rex. I've simply got to take it. And *The Blade* would like nothing better than to have its reporter goad us into making some sort of physical attack."

"I wouldn't make a physical attack. I'd just grab his coat collar and hustle him out into the corridor."

"And then what?" Selby asked, grinning.

"Then," Brandon said, his eyes suddenly gleaming with anticipation at the thought, "I'd haul off my right foot and see how far I could kick him."

"Exactly," Selby said, "and you know the way *The Blade* would write it up. It would be that the irate sheriff, trapped by evidences of his own stupidity, being unable to offer any explanation for the things he had done, resorted to physical violence on the person of a flyweight disabled veteran who was merely asking for an explanation of the bizarre actions of the power-crazed authorities.

"No, Rex, we're behind the eight ball and we've got to think our way out."

10

OTTO LARKIN, THE PAUNCHY CHIEF OF POLICE, LEANING backward to keep his balance, walked with short, cautious steps down the inclined ramp to the basement storage level of the Central Garage.

The man at the window of the control booth looked up, saw who it was, nodded, and said through the open window, "Good afternoon, Chief."

Larkin nodded. Shrewd, glittering eyes surveyed the garage as though expecting to uncover some clue by the mere intensity of his survey.

The garage attendant said, "Something I can do for you, Chief?"

"We had a murder last night," Larkin said importantly.

"So I read in the paper. Daphne Arcola."

"Daphne Arcola nothing! That was some pipe dream the *county* officers conjured up. *We* weren't in on that bull."

"You mean she wasn't the one who was murdered?"

"That's right. This dead girl came from Montana and had red hair. This Daphne Arcola has red hair and comes from Montana. That's how the mistake was made. Thank heavens *we* didn't make it."

"And this woman isn't dead?"

"The corpse is dead as hell. There's nothing dead

98

about Daphne Arcola. I guess *The Blade* is really going to pour it on the county officials tonight.

"Well, that's *their* hard luck. What I'm interested in now is finding a car that may have any bloodstains on the cushions. That's particularly true of transient cars. Now you folks have some trade that comes over here from the hotel, and . . ."

"They have the murder car already," the attendant said.

"Who has?"

"The sheriff and the D. A. The sheriff had a technical man down here making casts of the tires. I understand they're going to move the car to the county garage."

"What car?"

"It has an Illinois registration and belongs to Dorothy Clifton, I understand. She's visiting out at the Lennox place. Didn't the murdered woman put in a call to the Lennox place?"

"Not the *murdered* woman," Larkin said, "but the one who . . . Say, let's take a look at that car."

The garage attendant said, "Maybe I'm talking out of turn. I wasn't told to say anything about this. I . . ."

"What the hell do you mean, talking out of turn?" Larkin demanded. "You're talking to the Law."

"Well, it was the Law that put it in here."

"Get busy and show me the car."

The attendant led the way to the automobile. Otto Larkin looked it over carefully. "Belongs to Dorothy Clifton," he said, "and Dorothy Clifton is visiting with the Lennox family?"

"That's my understanding."

"That's mine too," Larkin said. "They had a burglary out there last night. I'm investigating that, too."

"Must keep you pretty busy."

"Sure does. . . . You say they made casts from these tires?"

"That's right."

Larkin bent over and owlishly examined the tires. Then he straightened, said, "Okay, I just wanted to check on it. Who brought it in?"

"She brought it in and then said she was turning the ticket over to the sheriff. After a while one of the deputies came down and had the ticket for the car, and went over it . . ."

"Search it for blood spots?"

"The way it looked to me, they searched the car for everything. Then they made casts of the tires."

"Those tire treads seem to match with tracks we found out at the scene of the murder," Larkin said importantly, "but don't say anything about this. Just keep it under your hat."

"Okay."

"Not to the newspapers. Not to anyone."

"I understand."

Larkin picked up speed in his stride as he puffed his way up the inclined ramp to the sidewalk where his car was parked. He jumped in, stepped on the starter, and drove to the big frame house on Chestnut Street.

He got out and pounded his way up the stairs, rang the bell.

The housekeeper who came to the door looked at him with tired eyes, and said, "Who'd you want to see?"

"I'll begin with Mrs. Lennox," Larkin said.

"She's in the living room. I'll let her know that . . ."

"I'll let her know myself," Larkin said, and pushed his way importantly into the living room.

Mrs. Lennox had been writing a letter at the antique writing desk. She looked up with nervously fluttering eyelids, saw the chief of police, and hastily put a blotter over the face of the letter.

"Why, good afternoon," she said. "I didn't know you were coming. You didn't telephone."

Larkin walked over to a chair and sat down. "What's this about Dorothy Clifton's car?" he asked abruptly.

"What about it?"

"That's what I want to know. What about it?"

"She drove out from Chicago. She had a little motor trouble, sort of a tuning-up job, I believe. It's a long drive, you know."

"So what did she do?"

"Took the car into the garage this morning, I believe."

"Where is she?"

"Upstairs in her room."

"Let's get her. I want to talk with her."

"I . . . I'm afraid I don't understand."

Larkin said, "If you'll get her down here, we may be able to clear up a lot of things."

Mrs. Lennox said, "Just a moment." She arose from the desk, started for the door, then turned back to pick up the blotting paper, fold the sheet of stationery on which she had been writing, put it in an envelope; and holding the envelope in her hand, stalked out of the living room.

As soon as she had left, Larkin jumped up from the chair, moved swiftly over to the writing desk, picked up the blotter, looked at it, saw that he could decipher nothing from the face of the blotter, put it back on the desk, went back to his chair, sat down, crossed his legs, and waited.

Within a few minutes, Mrs. Lennox and Dorothy Clifton returned to the living room.

"This is Dorothy Clifton," she said, "my older son's fiancée."

"How do you do?" Dorothy Clifton said.

"Mr. Larkin is the chief of police here," Mrs. Lennox explained.

"Yes, so you told me."

"What about your automobile?" Larkin asked.

Dorothy glanced swiftly at Mrs. Lennox, then pleadingly at the chief of police. "It's . . . it's in a garage."

"I saw it in the garage. What about it?"

"It . . . I drove out from Illinois, you know, and I . . ."

"You gave the parking ticket to the sheriff?"

"To the district attorney."

"Why did you do that?"

"They . . . I think they wanted to look the car over."

"Dorothy!" Mrs. Lennox exclaimed.

Larkin said, "The marks on your tires match the tire marks that were found at the scene of the murder."

"I . . . I was afraid . . ."

"What have you to say to that?"

"Nothing."

"How did your car get there?"

"I've explained that to the district attorney."

"Well, explain it to me," Larkin said.

Mrs. Lennox said frigidly, "*Really*, Dorothy."

Dorothy said, "I didn't see any reason for making a

102

scene about it. I don't know who was driving the car. I simply cannot identify the driver."

"What in the world are you talking about, Dorothy?"

"What driver?" Larkin asked.

"It was after I had gone upstairs," Dorothy said. "I had undressed and was standing by the window. I'd left my car so that it blocked the driveway. I felt that it was something of an imposition, but I understood none of the cars would be taken out of the garage until morning, so I . . . well, I still don't know who it was that drove the car."

"Dorothy, what on earth *are* you talking about?"

"And," Dorothy went on defiantly, "when I looked through the car, I found this purse."

"What purse?"

"A purse that evidently belongs to Daphne Arcola. I took it to the district attorney this morning."

"Why didn't you say something last night? Why wait until this morning?"

"I . . . I didn't realize it was important until this morning."

Larkin said, with heavy sarcasm, "*Your* story is now that someone took your car. You thought enough of it to sit up and wait until you saw what time the car came back. Then you went down and looked it over. You found a purse. You didn't say anything to anybody. . . . When was this, before the house was broken into or afterwards?"

"Before. Just before."

"What do you mean, just before?"

"I believe I know what she means," Mrs. Lennox said, as Dorothy hesitated. "When I heard the sounds of the screams, I ran to the head of the stairs. I was in time to

103

see Dorothy on the stairs, carrying a purse under her arm. She had turned and was running down the stairs, but I know absolutely she couldn't have left the corridor and gone downstairs. She must have been on her way up and then turned around . . ."

"That's right," Dorothy said, looking Mrs. Lennox squarely in the eyes. "I had gone down to look in my car. I had found the purse, and was coming back. I had started up the stairs. I was about a third of the way up when I heard the screams. I didn't know what to do for a moment. Then I heard your steps in the corridor, and so I turned and started down the stairs in the direction of the screams."

The silence that followed was heavy with suspicion as Mrs. Lennox glanced apprehensively at the chief of police, then hastily averted her eyes.

"So," Larkin said, "you were downstairs, right near Moana's bedroom where the burglary was committed at the very time the screams sounded?"

"I told you I was approximately a third of the way *up* the stairs."

"You'd been prowling around the house at night, and . . ."

"I had gone down to look over my automobile. I wanted to see . . . well, I wondered who had taken it."

"And you didn't tell the police any of these things?"

"No, why should I?"

"You told the district attorney this morning."

"Because then it appeared that the purse that was in my car belonged to the murdered woman."

"Dorothy, what are you saying!" Mrs. Lennox exclaimed sharply.

Larkin said, "And it looks as though your car was the car that was used by the murderer."

"I know nothing whatever about that."

"Who knows you were in your bedroom all the time your car was out?"

"No one, naturally," Dorothy said, with dignity. "A single, unmarried woman hardly keeps an alibi in her bedroom."

"Dorothy," Mrs. Lennox said acidly, "are you trying to convey the impression that some member of this family took your car without your permission?"

"*Someone* took it."

"Why didn't you say something? Why didn't you . . . ?"

"I thought at first my car was just being moved out of the driveway. Then when it was gone—well, I waited to see what time it came back. I naturally was curious."

"It's a shame that you didn't share your curiosity," Mrs. Lennox said.

"What was I supposed to do?" Dorothy asked.

"I don't think there's any need to discuss it at this time," Mrs. Lennox said, with frigid formality.

Dorothy got up to leave the room. "Under the circumstances, I assume you'll be happier if I go to the hotel."

"Just a minute, just a minute," Otto Larkin said heavily. "I'm not satisfied with your story—the one you have now."

"It's the same one I always had," Dorothy said. "I tried to spare embarrassment to the family of the man I love. If you want to ask me any more questions you may call on me at the hotel."

And she went swiftly out of the room leaving a cold, hostile silence behind her.

//

ENSCONCED IN HER ROOM IN THE MADISON HOTEL, DOROTHY
Clifton put in a long-distance call almost as soon as the
bellboy had closed the door behind him.

"I want to talk with Horace Lennox," she said,
"Horace Crittendon Lennox, L-E-N-N-O-X. He's an attorney at law in Chicago. I want to talk with him personally, and I want you to rush the call through. Just a
moment and I'll give you his number."

She was sufficiently upset so that she didn't trust her
memory, and looked in her notebook before giving the
operator the number. "Will you please try to rush it?"
she asked. "I'm Dorothy Clifton. I've just checked in
Room . . ." She looked at the placard on the telephone,
and said, "Room 310."

Downstairs at the moment in the hotel lobby, Otto
Larkin was flashing his badge on the operator. "You
have a new tenant in 310," he said. "I want a record
of every telephone call she makes, and I want you to
listen in on incoming calls so you can find out who's
calling. Now, that's an order direct from police headquarters."

"She has a call in now, Chief," the operator said.

"Who to?"

"An attorney in Chicago."

"Oh, oh, calling a mouthpiece, eh?" Larkin said. "Can you put me where I can listen in, and . . ."

"I'm sorry, that's against the rules and against the law. I couldn't do that for anyone or for any reason."

Larkin said, "Well, keep a list of the calls and the numbers."

He walked over to the telephone booth, dropped in a nickel, and dialed *The Blade*.

"Harry Elrod there?" he asked. "This is Larkin talking. . . . Okay, put him on.

"Hello, Harry? Got a story for you. The D. A.'s office and the sheriff are trying to pull a fast one. They're investigating the car that figured in that murder. But I took a short cut and got some admissions from the owner of the car that are damned important.

"Now, get this straight. Here's a juicy scandal. The car belongs to Dorothy Clifton, who was staying out at the Lennox house. She's supposed to be engaged to the oldest Lennox boy. She tells a weird story about someone taking her car, and then finding the purse of the girl who was supposed to have been murdered. I went after her and made her admit that she'd been downstairs at the exact time Moana Lennox caught someone prowling in her bedroom. Also, she could have been driving the car. Under the circumstances, Mrs. Lennox virtually kicked her out, and she's registered at the Madison Hotel. Just checked in. There should be a swell interview for you there, and, as far as I'm concerned, you can bust the story wide open. *The Clarion* never did anything for me. Just don't say who gave you the tip, that's all."

Harry Elrod was fawningly grateful, and Larkin, a pleased smile on his face, hung up the telephone, bit the end from a cigar, and walked out to the red police car which he had left parked halfway down the block.

Up in her room, Dorothy found herself pacing back and forth like some caged animal, as though the very nervous energy she was pouring out might in some way speed things up so that she could begin to get results.

Then the telephone rang, and the operator said, "Just a moment."

There was an interminable agony of suspense, during which Dorothy wondered if perhaps Horace might be out of town, and then the welcome sound of his voice came over the telephone.

"Hello, darling," he said, "I'm taking the words right out of your mouth so that we can save the preliminaries and devote as much of the three minutes as possible to having you reassure me as to my good fortune.

"You are mainly calling for the purpose of telling me that all of your fears have been groundless, that the Lennox family is really human, that my mother is treating you like the queen which you really are, and that you're having a good time, but are missing me. And are planning on getting back just as soon as possible.

"So now, having disposed of the preliminaries, we'll amplify that theme about how you miss me for the remaining two minutes and twenty-two seconds of our three-minute call."

"Horace," she said desperately, "you must catch the first plane and get out here."

"What's that?"

"The *first* plane," she insisted. "I'm no longer at your house. I'm at the Madison Hotel. I'm in Room 310, and it's terrible."

"Dorothy, what in the world has happened?"

"Everything."

"Do you mean you aren't getting along with the family?"

"I'm not getting along with the family. I'm not getting along with the chief of police. I'm afraid I'm about to be arrested for murder. I've been trying to cover up for someone in your family, and my name is going to be smeared all over the newspapers.

"Or, looking at it from your mother's standpoint, I have dragged the Lennox name into the mud, committed a murder, stolen the family heirlooms from Moana, and . . ."

"Dorothy, are you kidding?"

"I wish I were. It's a bad dream. Horace, I need you. Grab a plane and get out here."

"Dorothy, is this a gag to get me out there for some celebration or something? Remember that I'm a struggling young attorney, and having just opened an office . . ."

"Horace," she interrupted firmly, "I feel a strong sympathy for women who have hysterics. I've pinched myself black and blue, trying to convince myself it's some hideous nightmare. In short, as I have written so many times during my practice days on the typewriter, 'Now is the time for all good men to come to the aid of the party.'"

"The good men are coming," Horace announced. "We'll grab the first plane. Rest assured, Bright Eyes, that Sir Galahad is riding to the rescue."

"Not Sir Galahad," she said. "There are connotations of righteous virtue reeking about that character. What I need is someone who can take me in his arms and make me forget that I am being cast in the role of defendant by the local constabulary."

"Hold everything until I get there," he said. "I'm riding a white charger which will be all spotted with mud. I think the regularly scheduled planes will get me in to Los Angeles around six o'clock in the morning, your time, but I think there are some independent flights on which I can save a little money, and they'll leave whenever they have a load. Anyway, I'll come walking in on you. You'll be at the Madison Hotel?"

"Better inquire at the jail first."

She was reassured by his laugh, although she could detect a note of nervousness in his voice.

"You sit tight and hold everything, Princess. I'll be right out."

She hung up the phone with a feeling of relief.

12

REX BRANDON CALLED SELBY ON THE PHONE AND SAID, "Doug, I think we've finally got our corpse identified."

"Who is she?"

"Her name is Rose Furman. She has an apartment in Los Angeles, in the Pocahontas Apartments."

"How did you get the identification, Rex?"

"Through her shoes. She has a very narrow foot, and it's difficult for her to get shoes. This shoe store has been selling her shoes on special order for four or five years. They know her because they've delivered shoes to her apartment, and she has a charge account. Aside from that, they don't know much about her. Sometimes she'd come in and buy one or two pair of shoes, sometimes three or four pair. Then they wouldn't see her again for months. I'm going into L. A. Want to come along?"

"Sure," Selby said. "How about taking Sylvia along?"

"Sure thing."

Selby said, "Well, we'd better tip her off, and let her follow in her own car. We've been in enough trouble for one day taking reporters along with us."

"I'll say we have."

"I'll get hold of her," Selby said.

"How about it, Doug? If this looks like the girl, do we go in her apartment and look around?"

"We use our judgment. But before we make a move we'll have a complete identification. You have her picture. We'll get someone to identify the picture positively. Then, if we find out she's missing from her apartment, and we have a positive identification, and the man in the shoe store identifies the photograph, I see no reason why we shouldn't go in."

"It's okay by me," Brandon said.

"I'm getting a line on a little stuff here and there," Selby said, "but I . . ."

"Hey, wait a minute," Brandon interrupted, "something's happened. *The Blade* is out on the streets. It must be darned near forty minutes early. I can hear the newsboys screaming at the top of their lungs."

"Well," Selby said, "we'll see if . . ."

"Just a minute, here's one of the deputies. He's got a paper. . . . Oh, oh, Doug, this looks like *something!*"

"What is it?"

"That's why they wanted to get out on the streets and grab the credit," Brandon said. "Otto Larkin has grabbed the whole front page of the paper."

"What's he done?" Selby asked.

"According to the paper," Brandon said, "he's arrested the person who committed the murder, and . . . and damned if he hasn't arrested Dorothy Clifton, Doug . . . and *The Blade* claims he's found the murder weapon and bloodstained clothing in the suspect's hotel room . . . and there's merry hell to pay."

Selby said, "Throw the paper in the car, Rex. We'll read the lurid details on the way to Los Angeles."

13

the sheriff piloted the big county car over the Los Angeles highway.

"Well," he said, "we have to read *The Blade* to find out what Daphne Arcola was doing here. Listen to the statement she made to Harry Elrod. This is in quotes, Rex, as her story:

"During the latter part of July, the twenty-ninth to be exact, I found myself temporarily out of funds in Yuma, Arizona.

"A young chap offered to take me part way to Los Angeles which was my destination. He said he would drive until he got too sleepy to go on. His first name was Frank. He was driving a car with a Missouri license. I'm almost certain he said his last name was Grannis.

"He drove me as far as Madison City. He told me he was too sleepy to try to go on, and said he was going to stay at a motel. He was a perfect gentleman, and offered to get me a single room if I desired to wait and go on with him next morning. However, I couldn't do that, despite the fact that it was then well past midnight. I had to be in Los Angeles and decided I would hitchhike on through.

"A motorist gave me a ride within five minutes of the time Frank let me out of his car, and I didn't think any more of it until I read in the paper a Frank Grannis had been arrested in Madison City on a hit-and-run charge. I returned to Madison City to investigate, because if this Frank Grannis is the same man who gave me a ride to Madison City, I know he couldn't have been involved in any accident. I was with him from the time he left the checking station on the Arizona–California border until he turned in for the night at Madison City.

"This is the reason I came to Madison City. I wanted to investigate the hit-and-run case because I understood Frank Grannis was arrested here, then taken to some other county.

"Imagine my surprise when I awakened this morning to find the county officials not only had me listed as being murdered, but also calmly invaded my bedroom by the means of a passkey without so much as a knock on the door."

Brandon said, "Why, *I'm* the one who arrested that Frank Grannis, Doug. The highway police found this dead Mexican outside of Holtville. He'd evidently been riding a bicycle and a car had hit him, knocked him over into the ditch, and the driver had kept right on going. A piece of the headlight lens was found just to the side of the highway at the scene of the accident, and another piece a little farther over toward the ditch. The police telephoned all along the highway asking us to search transient garages and auto courts for a car with a broken headlight lens.

"I remember one of the deputies located this Grannis car. The headlight on the right-hand side was broken, there was a big dent in the fender on the right side and the man who owned the car admitted he had driven up from Tucson the day before, driving until late at night.

"I notified the El Centro sheriff and described the pieces of glass which were missing from the bent headlight. They seemed to check. So the El Centro men rushed up here bringing the pieces with them. There's no question about it. The pieces fitted absolutely. Grannis hit that Mexican.

"The El Centro authorities filed a hit-and-run charge against him and took him back with them."

"Well," Selby said, "you can see what's happened now. And here, of course, is something that shouldn't come as any *great* surprise."

"What's that, Doug?"

"The attorney who is representing Frank Grannis is Mr. Alfonse Baker Carr."

"Now why the devil didn't Daphne Arcola tell *you* that when you talked with her?"

"Hard to tell," Selby said. "Probably because Carr warned her not to tell me anything. We can begin to fit events into a pattern now. She must have got in touch with Carr very shortly after our talk with Mrs. Carr. That's why she was out until four o'clock in the morning. Old A. B. C. must have known, shortly after we left his house, that we'd made a mistake in identifying the corpse, but he never said a word about that. He just let us go ahead, let *The Clarion* publish the report of Daphne Arcola's death—and I suppose now he'll have Daphne Arcola file a suit against the newspaper."

"Damn him," Brandon said angrily. "He could have saved us a lot of trouble by just picking up the telephone and putting in a call to my office."

"Well," Selby said, "when you come right down to it, Rex, why should he try to save us any trouble? Simply by keeping his mouth shut he gave Daphne Arcola a swell chance for a damage suit against *The Clarion* certainly, and perhaps against us."

"Well, he'll have a hell of a time explaining his silence in front of a jury," Brandon said.

"Oh, no he won't, Rex. Carr's too smart to get caught in that trap. If Daphne Arcola starts an action you can bet that Carr won't be her attorney of record. He'll have some stooge bring that suit. Carr will be very sympathetic toward us and commiserate with us on our predicament. Don't worry about old A. B. C. getting caught *that* easy."

Brandon said, "Sometimes I feel that it would be worth what it would cost to smash him in the puss. I don't see how you manage to tolerate him, Doug. The guy seems to amuse you. He makes me see red."

Selby laughed, "Frankly, Rex, I *like* the scoundrel. He's such a suave, ingenious devil, and you have to admit the man has one of the most powerful personalities you've ever encountered. He's a consummate actor, and you never catch him in an actual outright lie. He's perfectly willing to let us deceive ourselves, but he almost never makes a false statement. It takes an artist to do the things Carr does."

"Oh, I suppose he's smart all right," Brandon said. "Any editorial in there, Doug?"

"Oh, sure," Selby told him. "It's smeared all over the editorial page. I guess I told you that Paden gave me a chance to come into camp, and then threatened me with all sorts of trouble in case I didn't play ball. This case seems to be made to order for him."

"Paden!" Brandon snorted. "That's another one of Carr's importations. Personally, I'd make a bet that Carr put up the money that was used to buy *The Blade*. Look at what's happening right under our eyes. When Carr first came to this county he was almost pathetic

116

in his humble desire to become a part of our community and get away from the things which go with a criminal law practice in the big city. He wanted to retire. Then he said his clients wouldn't let him retire.

"First thing anyone knew, he was doing tricky legal jobs for prominent people here and getting them under obligations to him, until now he's a regular clearing house of crime.

"Every once in a while you hear of some other prominent citizen who went to him with something that was very hush-hush.

"That's one thing about old A. B. C. He *can* keep his mouth shut. And he knows how to get a prominent person out of a scrape so there's no faintest suggestion of publicity. Every time he gets someone out of trouble, he has another ace in the hole, some other person on whom he can call for help whenever he needs something done locally. I tell you, the man's dangerous. However, let's hear what Paden has to say in his editorial. I presume he's adopted the lofty condescension of a big city intellect dealing with a bunch of rural boobs. Damn those sneering, sarcastic editorials!"

"Why read them, Rex? You know they'll roast you, so why not just . . ."

"Nope, I couldn't do that," Brandon interrupted, grinning. "Let's hear what old Paden has to say, Doug."

Selby folded the paper, said, "All right, Rex, here we go:

Once again we are forced to call to the attention of the taxpayers the utter incompetency of the sheriff and district attorney of this county. Regardless of what some may think, it is not a pleasant duty; but it is for the best interest of

117

the community that we comment on their handling of this last and latest crime.

It so happens that the murder was committed within the city limits, and the city police were on the job at approximately the same time the over-zealous, publicity-hungry county officials started working.

If the county officials had wanted the whole-hearted co-operation of the city police chief, it was theirs for the asking. But the county men, acting with characteristic high-handed disregard for conventional methods of procedure, ignored the city police, even to the extent of failing to communicate important clues.

The manner in which their efforts backfired is attested by the fact that a veteran attorney, who has probably forgotten more law than the district attorney ever knew, and who was getting courtroom experience when the man who now guides the legal destinies of Madison County was in his swaddling clothes, is even now studying the possibilities of litigation.

It is astonishing that Doug Selby, as district attorney, should have put himself in the position he now occupies. Not only did he announce to the press that a certain young woman had been murdered, but he then proceeded to invade the privacy of her bedroom, apparently inviting in a reporter of the servile *Clarion* to watch him pull a rabbit out of a hat—or, in this case, a clue out of a suitcase.

And just as soon as Sheriff Brandon could break away without letting the chief of police know where he was going, Brandon joined Selby at the hotel. There the two of them set about the systematic search of a room which had been rented by a young woman whose only similarity to the corpse was the fact that they both had been more or less recently in a Montana city.

But the point is that all of this unseemly haste, all of this invasion of privacy, all of this cheapening of the county, merely for the purpose of gaining individual credit, not only accomplished nothing, but did have a tendency to delay the solution of the case. It remained for Chief of Police Otto Larkin, working carefully and methodically, running down clues, putting two and two together, not only to make an arrest of a person who quite evidently is the guilty party, but to uncover evidence which is of the greatest importance, evidence which the county officials would never have seen had Larkin not been on the job.

And, as for a custom which has persisted for years in the office of the sheriff and district attorney, the habit of paying off political debts by catering exclusively to one newspaper and releasing news only through that most favored press organ, this is once when our esteemed contemporary has quite evidently outreached itself, and legal action is in the offing.

Brandon interrupted angrily, "It's the way they say those things that makes you so damn mad. You'd think we were standing at the Pearly Gates and Saint Peter was looking at us over the top of his glasses and telling us what we'd done wrong. What's all this new evidence Larkin got?"

Selby said, "Dorothy Clifton, after leaving the Lennox home, apparently by request, went to the Madison Hotel. She put through a phone call or two, then went out. Larkin searched the room. He found blood spots on a blouse in her suitcase. He took the blouse, rushed it to a laboratory. Tests showed the spots were human blood. Larkin made the arrest then. Dorothy Clifton says the blouse was one she wore crossing the divide where she had a nosebleed. She insists all the blood spots were from that nosebleed."

"And that's Larkin's whole case?" Brandon demanded. "Just the tracks of her car and spots of blood on a blouse?"

"No," Selby said thoughtfully. "He found the murder weapon, Rex."

"That's what he claims," Brandon said. "I'd bet money he hasn't. Where did he find it, Doug?"

"The newspaper says it is honor bound not to divulge that in print, but that once he was certain of his quarry, Larkin showed the tireless determination of a bloodhound in . . ."

"Skip all that, Doug. It makes me sick. For heaven's sake, Doug, are people that dumb?"

Selby smiled. "It depends on how a thing is presented to them, Rex. Of course, the mysterious recovery of this murder weapon makes the whole story ring true . . . if it *is* the murder weapon and Larkin has recovered it."

"If it's the murder weapon and Otto Larkin recovered it, I'll eat it," Brandon declared. "And now we have this Arcola woman getting mixed up with old A. B. C. in that El Centro hit-and-run case. . . . Well, we'll keep on ridin' and spurring, Doug, and see where *we* come out. . . . Won't Larkin have to turn that murder weapon over to us?"

"Oh sure," Selby said. "Now that he's had all the newspaper credit, he'll turn the whole thing over to us —dump it right in our laps, in fact."

Selby abruptly folded *The Blade* and tossed it over in the back of the car. "Let's go ahead and call the shots as we see them and just forget all about the opposition."

He pushed his hands down deep in his trousers pockets, and remained silent until Brandon swung the car off a main boulevard and said, "This is where we're to meet the sheriff's man."

A sheriff's car was waiting at the corner. Two men were in it. A deputy sheriff spotted Brandon's car, came forward, shook hands and was introduced to Doug Selby as Halbert Hardwick, a deputy who had worked with Brandon on other cases.

"We've been getting a line on this babe," he said, "and we've uncovered some funny stuff."

"What is it, Bert?"

"She was a dick."

"For the city?"

"No, a private dick. Ran a little agency of her own. One of the men in the department of records thought he remembered the name, so we looked her up. Sure enough, it was the one. She has a license and everything."

"What sort of work?"

"For the most part she specializes on cases involving playboys. She's rather a hot number when she decks herself out, and they say she twists them all around her finger and wrings them inside out."

"Well, she isn't going to do any more twisting," Brandon said. "She's dead. That is, if this is the one. If she was a private detective, we should be able to make an identification."

"Sure we can make an identification. We have everything, even her fingerprints. I brought the records along."

"Good work," Selby said. "We have prints of her fingers and a photograph."

Brandon opened his wallet, unfolded a set of fingerprints, and took out a photograph.

"Darned if it doesn't look like the same one," Hardwick said. "Let's take a look at those prints. I'll take the ring finger. You take the right forefinger, Sheriff."

"Sure looks the same," the sheriff announced, at length. "Of course, it isn't like making an absolute comparison, but . . ."

"It's the same, all right," Hardwick said. "Well, that makes it a cinch, Sheriff. I guess we have the identity all cleaned up right now. What's more we've got the man for whom she was working at the time she was bumped off."

"How did you do all that in such a short space of time?"

"Leg work and luck. This chap kept trying to contact her all last night. He had his car parked in front of the building all the first part of the evening, and then he showed up again before daylight this morning. The manager of the apartment house saw it was an out-of-state car and took his license number, just in case. So, when we got your phone call, we started checking up and when we came to the conclusion this girl was the one you were interested in, we started talking with the landlady. She told us about this car. She'd made a note of the license number. While we were talking, he drove up. Naturally, we started asking him questions. He's trying to play cagey. We haven't wanted to go really to work on him until you got here."

"What's his story generally?"

"You'd better get it firsthand," Hardwick said. "So far he hasn't given us much except that this Furman dame was doing something for him, and he's trying to contact her to find out what she's learned. We've got the guy parked over here in my car.

"His name is Barton Mosher. He lives up in Windrift, Montana. Come on over and get his story."

"Does he know anything about what we're investigating?" Selby asked.

The deputy flashed him a quizzical look, said, "We're not *that* dumb, Mr. Selby. That guy just knows we're looking for Rose Furman, and that's all. Come on over and meet him."

They walked over to the deputy's car.

Hardwick said to the man who was seated in the automobile, "These are a couple of friends of mine, Mr. Selby and Mr. Brandon. And this is Barton Mosher."

The men shook hands.

"Will someone kindly tell me what this is all about?" Mosher demanded.

"That's what *you're* going to tell *us*," Hardwick said. "Now, you've been hanging around Rose Furman's apartment, and . . ."

"I tell you it was simply a matter of business. I told you what it was."

"All right, tell us again. My friends might be interested."

"I asked Rose Furman to do something for me. I don't know as I should be telling all this," Mosher said.

"Suit yourself," Hardwick told him. "We can take you up to headquarters and let you think it over just as well as not. If you have anything to conceal, you'd be foolish to incriminate yourself."

"What do you mean, incriminate myself?"

Hardwick explained patiently, "I'll give it to you all over again. Concentrate on it, now. Rose Furman isn't home. She hasn't been around her apartment for a while. You've been hanging around there. You're acting mighty suspicious. The people in the neighborhood begin to wonder what it's all about. One of them telephones in. So we come out and ask you, and you start playing button, button, who's got the button with us."

"Say, what are you talking about? You fellows can't do this. I could go phone my lawyer."

"Come on, let's go down to headquarters and you can phone your lawyer from there."

"I don't want that. There are newspaper men hanging around police headquarters."

"Sure. You afraid of them?"

"Yes. That is . . . well, I can't stand . . . I don't want publicity."

"Maybe you'd like to talk here, then."

"My lawyer . . ."

"Keep on being cagey with us and you'll need a lawyer."

Hardwick yawned. "One of you guys got cigarettes? Guess we'd better go on down to the sheriff's office."

"Rose Furman is a detective," Mosher blurted, "and a good one. She's done work for me in the past, and has always done a very fine job."

"Go on, buddy. Keep talking."

"I live in Montana and, I'll be frank about it, I run a place there where I try to give the boys a little action, nothing too much out of the way, but a little blackjack, roulette, poker, and a few games of chance."

Mosher hesitated.

"Go on," Hardwick prompted. "You're started now."

"A couple of months ago, on the twenty-sixth of July, to be exact, a girl who hangs around and plays the dude ranches, came in and had a winning streak. It was a winning streak that looked mighty suspicious to me. She cleaned up about six thousand dollars. Now I could afford to lose that if everything was on the up-and-up, but a little birdie whispered in my ear that the deal might have been fixed up with one of my men. Of course, those boys are professionals, and it would be pretty hard to fix them. You couldn't do it with money, but this girl is quite a dish, and—well, I started wondering, that's all. Finally I decided I'd send a few hundred dollars along with the six thousand just to find out. So I got Rose Furman to try and locate this girl, and . . ."

"She'd left town?" Brandon interrupted.

"That's right. She dusted out the day after she made the winning. She was gone for perhaps two weeks or so, then she came back for a little while, and then she left again. The way she acted and everything, I was plenty suspicious."

"All right, what's the rest of it?"

"Well, Rose phoned me that she had a definite answer; that if I'd be here to meet her at her apartment she'd give me complete proof of what I wanted."

"And then she didn't show up?"

"She didn't show up. Now I happen to know she's working on another job which took her to Windrift, Montana. In fact, that's the reason I happened to think of her. She came walking in three or four weeks ago and said hello and told me she was working on a job; that it didn't concern me at all, but that she wanted to get some information from me about some of the other places and how they were being run. So I asked her if she could take on a job for me on the side, and she said she didn't see any reason why not. So I told her about this girl and about being nicked for the six grand. Now then, gentlemen, there's my story. I'm clean as a hound's tooth. I'll show you my driver's license, show you pictures of my place, and if I absolutely have to, I can give you references of people here in town who know me, people who have been staying out at one of the dude ranches around Windrift, and have had occasion to stop in at my place and naturally they've remembered me. I try to treat them right."

"Okay," Hardwick said, "let's take a look at what you've got, buddy. Turn your pockets out. Got any letters from this Rose Furman?"

"Certainly not. She didn't send me letters, and I didn't want any. When she had anything important she'd let me know on the phone. When I hire a detective there's only one thing important that I want and that's the final answer."

"Where're you staying in town?"

"At the Critchwood."

Hardwick glanced at Brandon and Selby, turned back to Mosher. "All right, buddy, you left out one of the answers."

"What's that?"

"The name of the lucky girl."

"I left that out on purpose."

"I'm asking her name on purpose."

"I don't see that it needs to enter into it."

"Why are you protecting her?"

"I'm not protecting her. I'm protecting me. We don't gossip about such things in my profession."

"You're not gossiping. You're answering questions. You're among friends—if you act friendly. Now then, what's her name?"

"She's a girl who plays the dude ranches."

"You told me that before. Now I want her name."

"Daphne Arcola."

Hardwick turned to the visiting officials. "That name mean anything to you boys?"

Brandon's nod was all but imperceptible.

"And Rose Furman told you she had the definite answer on this babe."

"That's right."

"Did she say whether it was good or bad?"

"No, just that she'd be ready to tell me the answer."

"Where'd she phone from?"

"Some place in the citrus belt. Madison City, I think it was."

"You fellows want this man any more now?" Hardwick asked. "We can let him go to his hotel and then check up on him by telephone. What's the name of the sheriff in your county at home, buddy?"

Mosher grinned and said, "I'll even go you one better than that. I'll give you one of his election cards when he was running last fall. I wish you'd ring *him* up and ask him about *me*."

"Okay, we will."

"You don't know where Daphne Arcola is now?" Selby asked.

"No, I don't, but I'm satisfied that Rose Furman does. If we can get hold of her she'll tell us the whole thing."

"You think Daphne Arcola put over a crooked play to win the six thousand?"

"I don't know. I was willing to spend a little money to find out, that's all."

Brandon said, "If your place was on the square, one of your men couldn't very well stand in on the deal so that he could make a pay-off."

Mosher looked at him, thought a moment, then said dryly, "I hadn't thought of that, gentlemen."

Hardwick chuckled. "All right, go to your hotel and stay there, now. Don't do any running around. We may want to talk with you. If we do, we want to be able to put our finger on you. That car's registered in your name?"

"That's right, that's my car."

"You drove it out here?"

"Yes, and it didn't take me very long. I came tearing right along. I'm nervous, and when I'm going any place I want to be the one who pushes the throttle."

"Then you feel Daphne Arcola is around here somewhere?"

"I think so. Rose Furman telephoned me to come to her apartment here. She said she was going to be in a position to give me an answer."

"What's the name of this man you think was standing in with her?"

"I'd rather not say. I have some good men there and if I make a bad guess it's going to . . ."

"Which one do you think?"

"I don't know. That's what I was getting Rose Furman to find out. I can stand a six-thousand-dollar loss—once. I'd hate to have to stand it twice."

"Okay," Hardwick said, "there's your car. Get in and drive it to your hotel."

Mosher smiled affably. "Well, gentlemen, I'm glad to see you, and if you're ever around Windrift, Montana, drop in at the Crystal Ball."

"You run wide open up there?" Sheriff Brandon asked.

Mosher grinned. "Not *wide* open, Sheriff, just open."

14

"YOU FELLOWS WANT IN THIS FURMAN APARTMENT?"
Hardwick asked.

"We want in," Brandon said. "But we don't want any
kickback."

"Leave that to me. We'll go in."

"When?"

"Now. The place is right around the corner."

"How about keys?" Selby asked.

"I got a passkey from the manager. It's all ready for
us to go in if we want."

Selby said, "I have a friend who's supposed to be waiting to meet us at the apartment, a newspaper
woman. . . ."

"Friendly newspaper?"

"Yes."

"Sure, bring her along," Hardwick said. "It's okay by
me. My instructions are to co-operate with you boys to
the limit. Whatever you want is what I want."

They rounded the corner and Sylvia Martin in her
car, seeing the three men walking toward the entrance
to the apartment house, gave Selby a tentative flashing
glance, then demurely lowered her eyes and turned her
head, taking the part of a modest young woman who,
while waiting for her escort to return, has yielded to
a brief flicker of curiosity.

"That your friend?" Hardwick asked.

Selby walked over and opened the car door. "It's all right, Sylvia," he said. "Miss Martin, may I present Bert Hardwick, of the local sheriff's office?"

"Glad to know you," Hardwick said. "Mr. Selby here says you're to come along, and these boys are running the show as far as we're concerned."

Sylvia smiled her thanks, and the four of them entered the apartment house and without even pausing at the manager's office climbed up two flights of stairs to the apartment Rose Furman had rented.

Hardwick inserted the passkey and opened the door, then stood to one side.

Rex Brandon entered the room. Doug Selby followed, then Sylvia Martin, and after them came Hardwick who closed the door behind him.

Brandon said, "I'm going to ask you to stand over in a corner, Sylvia, and not touch anything. Keep your eyes open, but let Doug and me make the search."

It was a two-room apartment. The living room had been fitted up as an office with a typewriter, a small safe, and a cabinet containing stationery. A waste basket by the small desk was cleaned out so that there was not so much as a crumpled piece of paper on the bottom. The typewriter, however, was open on the desk, and there was a piece of paper in it as though the occupant of the apartment had been interrupted in the midst of a letter and forced to leave upon some urgent matter of business.

Hardwick, Brandon and Selby, moving in concert, walked over to the typewriter.

The document was addressed to Barton Mosher, and was headed "Final Report."

Have completed investigation. The six thousand winning on July twenty-sixth was partially on the level, but you had better fire the man at the second roulette table. He is the one who has the little finger of his right hand off at the second joint.

The subject had to go to Los Angeles in July. She was broke at the time. She made a deal with this fellow to let her start with twenty-five-cent bets and run her winnings up to five hundred dollars. She had ten dollars as a starter.

I don't know how well you control your wheels. I am assuming you can pretty well control the *segment* but not the actual pocket in which the ball comes to rest. Therefore, odds can be made very decidedly against a person or very decidedly in that person's favor but that's all.

Your employee kept his agreement. Things were manipulated so the subject stood a good winning chance. She lost about five dollars out of the ten she had to invest before she started to win. She had a few losing streaks but ran winnings up to the five hundred dollars. Her friendly dealer then gave her the signal to quit.

She took the five hundred, went over to one of the other tables and despite the fact that she had no understanding with the croupier she made a heavy killing.

A man named Carl Remerton was playing at that table. He dropped about fifteen grand in the course of the evening. Your man couldn't control the situation with two big players as long as they kept at opposite ends of the board. The subject was smart enough to know that and so this dealer (who was on the square) had to take his choice of big money from Remerton and letting the subject win up to six grand, or standing a chance of losing heavily to Remerton in order to stop the subject's winning.

This is the dealer whom you thought might be in on a crooked play with the girl since she made her big winnings at his table. Actually, the sole fix was with the dark-haired, blue-eyed dealer on the second roulette table to the left of the door, the one with the partly amputated little finger.

The subject was acquainted with Remerton which made it easy for her to play along. She kept gambling as long as Remerton did and left with him, which caused some people to think they were together.

Subject took the trip to Los Angeles and for some reason started hitchhiking with hard luck story despite heavy winnings. Hitchhiked from Yuma with Frank Grannis who took her as far as Madison City. She waited over about ten minutes in Madison City for another ride, then came on to Los Angeles. She has talked some about Frank Grannis. He was arrested on hit-and-run and she is in a position to give an alibi, but for some reason is playing the alibi story very close and doesn't want to go to the authorities in El Centro. She is making the approach through Grannis's lawyer who lives in Madison City.

Subject is now in Madison City and because of my presence there on this job have been asked to take over another job of greatest importance which will necessitate return to Madison City. I am typing this and waiting for this new client to pick me up. Hope you arrive before I have to return to Madison City, but if this client should come to pick me up before your arrival, I will leave this report at your hotel and will telephone you at your hotel. This job in Madison City is big . . ."

And there, in midsentence, the report ended.

Selby, Brandon, and Hardwick bent over the typewriter studying the report.

"Well, that's as far as she got," Hardwick said. "Someone came and picked her up. Someone who was in one hell of a hurry. You note that she'd promised to complete this report and send it to Mosher at his hotel. She didn't have time to do that. She didn't even have time to finish the sentence. Whatever hustled her off to Madison City was something important and mighty urgent. And her client was calling for her. She didn't call Mosher at the hotel, and he didn't hear anything from her because she was dead. She must have been killed within a very short time after she arrived in Madison City."

"Now," Brandon said, "let's start finding out how she got to Madison City. That may be important."

"Her car's down in the parking lot that's reserved for tenants of the apartment house," Hardwick said. "We've covered that. She didn't go in her car."

Selby said, "It would be interesting to find out just what she was working on. She was originally in Windrift on another job. Then Mosher hired her. That job took her to Madison City and while she was there she got in touch with someone who wanted her for a job of considerable importance.

"She evidently insisted that she return here to make a complete report to Mosher before she returned to Madison City. When she returned to Madison City she was to ride with her new client—not in her own car. Why?"

"Probably," Hardwick said, "because she was to go on an undercover job where she'd be with someone as a friend or relative or something of that sort. The car's registered in her name and would be a giveaway."

"Let's look around," Selby said.

Sylvia Martin said eagerly, "We could see whether she had any clothes with her. Apparently she didn't, Doug, and . . . there's a purse over on that desk."

Selby said to Hardwick, "One of the strange things about the case was that there was no purse found by the body of the murdered woman. That set us all off on a false lead."

Hardwick opened the purse on the desk. "This looks like the one she must have been carrying. It has her driver's license and all that in it. I tell you she was going on an undercover job and she didn't want to have a thing on her that would disclose her identity."

"Now, who the devil would hire a woman private detective in Madison City, Doug?" Rex Brandon asked.

Selby shook his head.

"I don't suppose she was foolish enough to leave books containing a list of her clients around the apartment," Brandon said. "And yet she must have kept *some* books."

"She was pretty cagey from all we could find out about her," Hardwick said. "Played them *very* close to her chest. The most logical person whom you'd expect to hire a private detective is a lawyer. You got any lawyers out there who go in for private detectives?"

Selby gave the matter frowning consideration, then shook his head.

"You sure got *one* out there," Hardwick said, grinning. "Doesn't old A. B. Carr practice out in your bailiwick now?"

"More or less," Brandon said stiffly.

"He's supposed to have retired, or be trying to retire," Hardwick went on. "That's a laugh. That guy has a finger in a lot of things. He's acquired enough influence around here so he very seldom shows up in court any more. He very seldom has to. The way he can fix things is a caution."

Selby said, "His wife knew Daphne Arcola. Seems peculiar that there'd be so many coincidences involving him."

"They're not coincidences with him," Hardwick pointed out. "It's what you might call a law of cumulative recurrence. You start doing business with a bank, and first thing you know it'll turn out that Carr got the banker's son out of a scrape two years ago and the banker is very anxious to see that Carr is kept satisfied. You get mixed up in a real estate deal and you'll find that Carr kept one of the brokers from losing his license a year ago last September, and when you get into court . . . well, I guess I'd better stop right here. Only don't think that little things are a coincidence when you're having dealings with that fellow. You cross his back trail everytime you start walking. That's not coincidence. It's because he gets around."

Brandon said, "I'd like to put him where he wouldn't get around so much."

"Who wouldn't," Hardwick retorted. "Didn't you fellows pretty nearly have him nabbed awhile ago?"

"He married the prosecution witness, or the one whom we would have had to call as the prosecution witness," Brandon said.

"Oh, that's right," Hardwick chuckled. "I remember now. I heard something about that. Well, what do you want to do here, fellows?"

"I'd give a lot to find out just who she's been working for," Selby said. "That other job she was on in Windrift, Montana, might mean something."

"I may be able to help you on that one," Hardwick said.

"I doubt if she left any documentary evidence lying around here in her apartment," Selby pointed out. "She was evidently away for days at a time and she certainly was too smart . . ."

"I didn't bank on that," Hardwick said. "There's one other angle that might help."

"What's that?"

"The telephone. There's a switchboard down here and they charge by the call. I told the manager downstairs to have a list prepared of all the telephone numbers she had been calling in the last two or three weeks. The manager hated to do it, but she finally came around. Just a second and I'll call the manager. She should have the list ready and I'll make a quick check for repeat numbers."

Hardwick went over to the telephone, talked with the manager a few minutes, then hung up, said over his shoulder, "Okay, boys, I'll call the office. I think I can have some information for you in just a minute. I have a telephone number that she's been calling a few times lately. Let me call the office and I'll translate that into a name and an address and we can start working from there."

Hardwick called the office and held the phone. After a few moments he said, "Okay, boys. The party we want is Mrs. Barker C. Nutwell at the Willington Apartments. They're out on Western Avenue. Want to finish looking around here, and then take a look at Mrs. Nutwell?"

"There's darn little to find here," Brandon said. "She must have carried most of her business in her head. Look at that report she was making in the typewriter. She didn't even put in a sheet of carbon paper for so much as a single carbon copy, and there isn't a filing case in the apartment. Even the wastebasket is cleaned slick as a whistle."

"I know," Hardwick said. "The manager said she didn't even get her mail here. . . . Let's go talk with this Nutwell party. She may know something."

"You have the address on Western?" Selby asked.

"I have it," Hardwick said. "Let's all go in my car. I know the short cuts and which intersections I can go through without slowing down."

"You can slow down for all of them, as far as I'm concerned," Brandon said. "We're not in that much of a hurry."

"We probably aren't at that. How about the reporter?"

Sylvia Martin looked pleadingly at Doug Selby.

"She comes," Selby said.

"Okay, you're the boss. We'll all go in my car. Let's get started."

The low drone of the siren moved into higher frequencies until it became a peremptory scream as the big car split its way through traffic, rocketed through red lights, passed up boulevard stops, and swung around streetcars.

Within a matter of minutes, Hardwick brought the car to a stop in front of the Willington Apartments and two minutes later they were knocking on the door of an apartment.

They heard slow, shuffling steps, the *thump-thump-thump* of a cane. Then the door was opened a crack until the safety chain locked it in position.

Skeptical gray eyes peered out at them with cold hostility from a wrinkled face.

"Mrs. Nutwell?" Selby asked.

"That's right. Who are you? What do you want?"

"I'm Mr. Selby, the district attorney of Madison County. And this is Rex Brandon, the sheriff of Madison County, with me. This other gentlemen is Mr. Hardwick, of the sheriff's office here."

Hardwick pulled back his coat so she could see the badge which he was wearing.

"Well, what do you want?"

"We want to talk with you."

"You're talking."

"We'd like to have more privacy."

"You've got all you need."

"Some of the things we have to say are confidential."

"Not as far as I'm concerned."

"Very well, then. Why did you employ a private detective? And when did you last hear from her?"

The gray eyes surveyed Selby's face in careful appraisal. "You fooled me at first," she said. "Looked too soft to be a district attorney. I guess you're all right. Who's that girl there?"

"A friend of mine," Selby said.

"Where's she from?"

"Madison City."

"Well, all right, I guess it's okay for you to come in. Come on."

She loosened the chain on the door, then stood to one side, and opened the door.

The four visitors filed in, and Mrs. Nutwell closed the door, slipped the safety chain into catch, then turned the bolt on the door.

She was a woman in the late sixties, evidently afflicted with rheumatism, and her bony hand clutched a cane which she used as she walked, but there was a birdlike dexterity about her, a quickness, and a deft assurance with which she planted the cane on the floor, which made her seem surprisingly light of foot.

The apartment was spacious and apparently consisted of several rooms. It was well furnished, with an abundance of deep, comfortable chairs, spread about in advantageous positions as though Mrs. Nutwell was accustomed to entertaining rather large groups of friends and was anxious to see that they were all comfortable.

"Sit down," she said. "Guess you can all find chairs. Pick a comfortable one. *I* like to be comfortable when *I'm* sitting down. My old bones are getting pretty sore, and I have to sit in comfortable chairs. Do a lot of reading and don't like to keep thinking about how I'm feeling when I'm reading. Want to forget about myself. Used to want to think about myself all the time—that's when I was young. Now I want to forget myself every time I can for as long as I can. Getting harder to do all the time. Well, somebody better start talking."

She settled herself in a chair, looking from one to the other with quick, eager, birdlike twists of her head.

Selby leaned forward in his chair. "We're trying to find out something about why you got in touch with Rose Furman, and just what you know about her."

"That's my business."

"Unfortunately," Selby said, "events have made it our business."

"What sort of events?"

Hardwick said, "Suppose you just answer our questions for a while, Mrs. Nutwell, and then we'll explain to you why we want the information."

"And suppose I *don't?*" she snapped. "Don't try to browbeat me, young man!"

Selby said, "We're not here out of idle curiosity, Mrs. Nutwell."

"I s'pose that's right. It ain't idle, but it's curiosity just the same."

There was silence for several seconds.

"Well," she demanded truculently.

Selby said patiently, "We'd like to know about why you hired Rose Furman."

"Who says I hired her?"

"We have reason to think you did."

"Well, if she's been talking, I'll certainly do something about *that*."

"She hasn't been talking," Selby said.

"Well, it looks mighty queer to me. Can't blame a body for being suspicious. Here you folks come up here and start trampling all over me. What's wrong with hiring a detective? S'pose I did? What's a detective for?"

"That's what we'd like to know," Selby said.

"Find out things for a body, I guess. Guess a person has a right to get information."

Selby nodded.

"Why do they let detectives carry on their profession if it's illegal to hire them?"

"It isn't," Selby reassured her, "but for certain reasons we're trying to check up on Rose Furman."

"What reasons?"

Selby held the gray eyes. "Rose Furman is dead."

The woman in the chair gave a quick, convulsive start. "What's that you say?"

"She's dead."

"Young man, you aren't lying to me?"

"I'm telling you the truth."

"How'd she die?"

"She was murdered."

"Who killed her?"

"That's what we're trying to find out."

"Sounds like a cock-and-bull story to me."

There was another interval of silence. Hardwick started to say something but Selby flashed him a warning glance, and the deputy lapsed into silence.

"Well, what do you want to know?" Mrs. Nutwell demanded again.

"How you happened to hire her, and what you know about her."

"Well, under the circumstances, looks as though you might be entitled to ask a question or two. I hired her on account of my brother."

"What about your brother?"

"That's what I'm trying to find out."

"How did you happen to hire her?"

"Well, I looked around a little bit. I wanted to get some private detective I could trust. I'd heard a lot about them. Some of them are good, some of them ain't worth a snap of your finger. Some of them string you along, make all sorts of reports aimed to keep you spending money until they bleed you white. Didn't want that kind. Wanted someone that would do the job quietly and competently. That's the trouble with people nowadays. They just ain't competent. Can't get anybody to dig in and really *do* a job."

Selby nodded. "And how did you happen to find Rose Furman?"

"Friend of mine told me about her. She doesn't send in reports. Sends a telegram once in a while, but gets results. She's quiet and keeps in the background. Doesn't want a lot of people knowing she's a detective.

Just has a certain trade and for the most part handles business for women. Leastwise, that's what I found out about her when I investigated and, believe me, I *did* investigate. Never was a person to go around throwing money to the birdies, giving it to people I didn't know anything about. They'll fool you, all of them."

"So you looked her up pretty carefully?"

"You bet I did."

"Now what was there about your brother that . . ."

"My brother died," she interrupted. "I didn't like what they said about the way he died. Didn't sound right to me. He was my younger brother, Carl Remerton. I'm a widow. Married Barker Nutwell when I was eighteen but he died six or seven years ago. My brother Carl's wife also died. We always were pretty close. He understood me and I understood him. Seven years younger than I am. Wanted to be a playboy after his wife died. Told him he was a damned fool. Leave that gallivanting around to the younger folks.

"Well, he'd worked hard all his life. No play. Just keeping his nose pushed right down against the grindstone all the time. Made money, but what good did it do him? Made lots of money. People with money aren't happy. Trouble with having money is you get to depend on money. People who are happy are the ones who have friends.

"When you get money, everyone wants to take it away from you. You have to stand guard over it all the time. Get a little bit careless with it, and you're right back to where you were in the first place, poor as a churchmouse. Put in all of your time trying to stand between people and your money, and what does it get you? Nothing but ulcers and blood pressure. But I couldn't talk to Carl. He wouldn't listen. He was a worker, that boy. Certainly did dig in and work all his life—partially due to his wife. Ain't going to say anything against her. Made up my mind I wouldn't when he married, and I never did, and ain't going to begin now."

She clamped her lips in a firm straight line and glared at her visitors in grim silence.

"Yes, I can understand," Selby said, reassuringly, "but, without saying anything against his wife, you can tell us that after she died your brother began to take life a little easier."

"Of course he did. You should have seen the change in him. Of course he missed her and he did a little grieving but actually it was just like a weight had dropped off of him. Made a big change in him—too much of a change. He never could do things by halves. He started playing just like he worked."

"Women?" Selby asked.

"How do I know," she snapped. "I didn't go spying on him."

Selby was contritely silent, and, after a moment, she said, "Carl always loved to play poker, gamble, bet on the horses, things like that. He wanted life, gaiety, wanted to go around to night clubs, watch them dance. Get out there on the floor and do a right smart bit of dancing himself. Foolish for a man his age to do it. He'd just turned sixty. A man had ought to start taking care of himself then. Your heart gets tired. Even if it doesn't tell you about it, it's still tired. Go pouring a lot more work on it, dancing around a crowded floor in air that's loaded with alcohol, perfume and tobacco, and there ain't any good going to come of it. Well, that's what he wanted, and that's what he got."

"Did he have any children?"

"Not a chick. I'm his only living relative."

"And therefore you inherited the money?" Selby asked.

"What do you mean by that?"

"I just asked."

"Of course I did. That is, I will. What about it?"

"Nothing."

"All right, then, nothing."

"Can you tell me more about your brother's death?"

"He went to this dude ranch up in Windrift, Montana, and I don't know what he was doing up there. Never tried to find out. Never cared. I suppose he was frolicking around and trying to have a good time, and if that's the way he wanted things, why that's the way he wanted them, and that's that.

"But when he died, he died pretty suddenlike, and when I started checking up on things I started looking for a bunch of traveler's checks he carried with him all the time. They'd been cashed. Just a day or two before he died he'd started cashing checks, quite a lot of checks, not too many, but quite a lot."

"How many?" Selby asked.

"Ten or fifteen thousand dollars, somewhere around in there. I can't remember the exact amount, thirteen thousand and something, I think it was."

"All the checks he had with him?"

"No, not all. He carried twenty thousand dollars in checks with him wherever he went. This was his way of being independent. That was his way of showing that he could do whatever he wanted to.

"Land sakes, life isn't made that way. People can't do what they want to. People are always doing what they don't want to do. That's the way life works, and don't ask me why. It's just the fact that you can't develop none by doing only the things you want to do. You do the things life makes you do, and somehow or other it seems to work out all right. But you take people who are in a position where they can do whatever they want to, and first thing you know they don't know what they want to do, and then they get sort of goofy. Leastwise, that's the way it seems to me."

"So you hired this detective to go and find out what your brother had been doing?"

"Hired this detective to go find out what caused my brother to cash those traveler's checks, and find out a little more about how he died. Doctors said his heart just gave way. Well, that's all right. His heart wasn't as strong when he was sixty as it was when he was twenty, but I just wanted to check up. Just wanted to satisfy myself. Wanted to find out what had happened to him."

"And did you?"

"Well, I found everything was all right. Leastwise, that's what that detective wired me."

Mrs. Nutwell got up from the chair, tapped her way across the room to a writing desk, opened it, and took out a yellow Western Union envelope. She removed the telegram from the envelope and handed it to Selby.

Selby said, "This telegram was sent from Corona at nine-thirty Tuesday night, and reads: HAVE FINISHED INVESTIGATION IN MONTANA. YOUR BROTHER ALTHOUGH OBVIOUSLY A FINE MAN WAS LEARNING ABOUT LIFE THE HARD WAY. HAVE MADE COMPLETE INVESTIGATION AND EVERYTHING IS ALL RIGHT. NIGHT BEFORE HE DIED DROPPED

145

FIFTEEN THOUSAND GAMBLING. GAME WAS RIGGED. HAD LOST FIVE THOUSAND TO CROOKED CARD SHARK WEEK BEFORE AND A GIRL HAD TAKEN HIM FOR FIFTEEN HUNDRED AS A QUOTE LOAN UNQUOTE. ALL REPORTS INDICATE HE WAS ENJOYING HIMSELF ENORMOUSLY BUT EXCITEMENT AND TENSION POSSIBLY PRECIPITATED HEART ATTACK. WILL REPORT TO YOU IN DETAIL WITHIN NEXT DAY OR TWO. IN THE MEANTIME HAVE TO STOP OFF MADISON CITY ON ANOTHER MATTER WHICH WILL ONLY TAKE ABOUT TWENTY-FOUR HOURS.

SIGNED ROSE FURMAN

Selby said, "May we take this telegram, Mrs. Nutwell?"

She hesitated, then said, "Well, I guess it's all right. You say she was murdered?"

"That's right, apparently within two hours after she sent this wire. It seems she returned to Los Angeles, started to type out a report on another case, was interrupted by some client who called for her and insisted she leave immediately for Madison City with him—and she must have sent you this wire on the road to Madison City."

"And you don't have any idea who did the killing?"

"No, that's what we're trying to find out."

"She was a mighty competent young woman. She certainly knew her way around. Knew about life and about people. I talked with her. She told me she wouldn't send me in any report; that she didn't do business that way; that she took a case and went out and made a job of it. When she was finished she had the story. She told me she wasn't going to go running up a lot of expenses on me, but that I'd just have to sort of trust her. I felt certain she'd come back with the whole story and tell it to me all at once. She said reports just cramped her style.

She said she didn't want to have to start making guesses before she had all the facts."

"How long ago did you hire Rose Furman?" Selby asked.

"Must have been three or four weeks."

"And you gave her money?"

"I gave her four hundred against expenses. I agreed to pay her another four hundred for a complete report, where Carl went the last few days of his life, whom he was with and all that. If you find any notes she made on that, I want 'em.

"And," Mrs. Nutwell added, with sudden conviction, "you won't find any. She was too smart to have left as much as the scratch of a pen. You want to bet, young man?"

"No," Selby said, "I don't want to bet."

Sylvia Martin quietly slipped her folded notes back in her purse. She had her story.

15

DRIVING BACK TO MADISON CITY, SELBY STUDIED THE MYS-
tery of Rose Furman with frowning concentration and
Brandon refrained from interrupting the young district
attorney's thoughts.

It was as they were approaching Madison City that
Selby said, "Rex, we're confronted with a peculiar pattern. It isn't a pattern of coincidence and it isn't a pattern of accident."

"What is it, then?"

"Let's begin with Daphne Arcola," Selby said. "She
came to Madison City. Why?"

"The way it looks now," Brandon said, "it's because
she knew Frank Grannis had been arrested here and
then taken to El Centro."

Selby said, "The thought keeps recurring to my
mind, Rex, that Daphne may have gone to Madison
City because of the letter Babe Harlan wrote telling her
that she had married A. B. Carr."

"And she came to visit her friend?"

"Not to visit Mrs. Carr, but to consult A. B. Carr.
And that would explain that wire. Don't forget, Rex,
that Mrs. Carr mentioned something in her letter about
her marriage and the peculiar circumstances in connection with it; but then went on to state that her husband
was a wizard as a criminal attorney and that crooks who

were wise would wink at each other and say, 'It's as simple as A. B. C.' "

Brandon thought that over until they had turned into the main street of Madison City. Then he said simply, "Doug, that's the right track. Where do we go from there?"

Selby said, "We go to your office, and we call up the sheriff's office at El Centro. Then we drive down there and start sweating Frank Grannis to see if he doesn't have some of the answers we want."

Brandon said, "Sounds reasonable to me."

They turned off the main street and up the hill toward the Courthouse. Sylvia Martin's headlights were dancing along right behind them.

"Sylvia's making good time with that red buzz buggy of hers," Brandon said.

They parked their car at the Courthouse and waited for Sylvia. The three of them walked up the echoing marble steps to the sheriff's office.

The night deputy said, "This gentleman has been waiting to see you, Sheriff."

Brandon turned around as a tall, slim young man with worried eyes came up out of the chair in which he had been sitting and moved toward the sheriff with outstretched hand.

"You may not remember me, Sheriff," he said. "I knew you several years ago. I'm Horace Lennox. I . . ."

"Oh, yes," Brandon said. "You've been in Chicago, opened a law office there, I believe."

"That's right. I . . . I have a favor I want to ask you, Sheriff."

"What?"

"You're holding Dorothy Clifton, my fiancée, in jail.

149

I've flown out here to see her, and—well, I've run up against red tape on visiting hours and . . ."

The sheriff frowned dubiously, said, "Well, of course, right at this hour the prisoners are all asleep, and . . . probably first thing in the morning . . . I wouldn't hold you to visiting hours, but . . ."

Sylvia Martin, moving around behind the sheriff, tugged frantically at his coattails in a series of quick telegraphing jerks.

Brandon looked back over his shoulder at her, then suddenly grinned and added, "However, under the circumstances, Horace, I guess you're entitled to have most of the rules set aside. I guess Dorothy would be willing to be wakened in order to see you."

He turned to his deputy. "Get the matron on the phone. Tell her we're sorry to wake her up, but it's important that Dorothy Clifton have a visitor, and . . ."

Lennox grabbed Brandon's hand gratefully. "Sheriff," he said, "you'll never know what this means to me. I caught a night plane and . . . I know Dorothy is lying awake over there waiting for me. I told her I'd get here just as soon as I possibly could."

"You've seen your family?" the sheriff asked, conscious of Sylvia Martin's breathless eagerness.

"Yes, I came here and was told that I couldn't do anything until you returned, so I went out to the house and talked with my mother. She's very bitter. And I talked with Steve who's inclined to be reasonable, if it wasn't for Mom's influence."

Sylvia Martin stepped forward. She said, "I've never met you, Mr. Lennox, but I'm Sylvia Martin, of *The Clarion*."

Lennox suddenly became cautiously dignified. "Oh, yes," he said.

"And," Sylvia went on, "our opposition paper, *The Blade,* is trying to make it appear that Dorothy Clifton is guilty of this crime and *I'm* absolutely certain that she isn't. I'd like to have an interview with you after you've seen Miss Clifton, and see that—well, that her side of the story gets properly presented to the public. The fact that you've had enough faith in her to—well, you know, the general understanding is that *all* the members of your family don't feel the same way, and . . ."

She broke off to let a pleading smile finish the sentence for her.

Horace Lennox said, "Few people understand the situation. The family, of course, are very nervous and —well, you might say, hysterical. I don't think they're in a position to have any real perspective as yet. I sympathize with them but their outlook is . . . well, the chief of police here has completely pulled the wool over their eyes."

Sylvia Martin slipped her hand in the bend of Horace Lennox's arm, gently piloted him to one side. "While the sheriff and the district attorney are having a conference," she said, "and during the few minutes that it will be necessary to wait before the matron can get Dorothy ready to see you, I'd like to have you amplify that statement just a little so I can explain to my editor . . ."

Brandon, taking the hint, grinned at Selby, said, "Well, let's go put through that telephone call, Doug."

They retired to the inner office. Brandon rushed

through an emergency call to the sheriff's office at El Centro.

"Hello," he said, "this is Rex Brandon, sheriff of Madison County, talking from Madison City. You're holding a Frank Grannis down there, and we want to come down and talk with him. We'll be down just as soon as. . . . What's that?"

The sheriff listened for a matter of nearly a minute, then said, "Well, I guess that settles it then. Who did you say this fellow was? . . . I see . . . I see. All right, thanks."

The sheriff hung up the phone, turned to Doug Selby. "Well," he said, "*that* does it."

"What is it?" Selby asked.

"Late this afternoon," Brandon said, "counsel for Frank Grannis managed to get bail for his client reduced to three thousand dollars, and within thirty minutes surety bail was furnished by a 'friend' of the accused."

"Who was the friend?" Selby asked.

"The friend," Brandon said, dryly, "was a man whom the sheriff says he's satisfied Frank Grannis had never seen before in his life, but he put on a good act of back-slapping cordiality. As soon as Grannis was admitted to bail, this friend loaded him in an automobile and whisked him out of the country."

"The attorney, of course, was old A. B. C.?" Selby asked.

"That's right."

Selby put tobacco in his pipe, said, "Well, Rex, as the game starts flushing out of cover we begin to get more of a pattern."

"It isn't flushing *out* of cover," Brandon said. "It's getting *into* cover."

"Well, let's ring up that great super-sleuth, Otto Larkin, and find out about the murder weapon."

Brandon picked up the telephone, grinned as he said, "Get me Otto Larkin. Tell him I want him up here. Tell him if he has any evidence in that murder case to bring it up."

Brandon hung up the phone and said, "At least *The Clarion* will be able to run the story in the morning edition showing that we've identified the corpse and perhaps with an innuendo or two about the mysterious case on which this detective was working when she was murdered. That will give the other side something to worry about."

Selby nodded, looked at his watch, and said, "I'll bet Otto Larkin would like to cross the next half-hour right out of his life."

16

OTTO LARKIN'S WIDE-EYED, CHERUBIC INNOCENCE FAILED
to hide his embarrassment.

"Gosh," he blurted, "I didn't know I was going to run
into a deal of that sort. I guess I just got caught in a
political squeeze play, and . . ."

"What about this murder weapon?" Brandon interrupted.

Larkin eased his ponderous frame into a chair. Eager
affability oozed out of him like the perspiration on his
palms. "Now, look, fellows," he said, "I *tried* to get in
touch with you on that but it was a last-minute development."

"And so you got in touch with *The Blade* instead?"
Brandon asked.

"It just happened that they had a man in touch with
me, and—well, I didn't know just *what* to do. I thought
if I held out on them we'd make them hostile and—
well, you know how it is. There isn't a case against
Dorothy Clifton except for that murder weapon. Of
course, we have bloodstains and it was her car that was
in the park, and all that, but—well, you know, I don't
want to go off half-cocked."

"Well, *what* about the murder weapon?" Selby asked.

"Well, you see it was this way, fellows. I covered the
garages looking for the murder car and of course I

spotted this one and learned it belonged to Dorothy Clifton, so I thought I'd go talk with her. As soon as I talked with her, I knew that she was concealing something, so I put a little pressure on her and found out about her wild story that the car had been taken the night before. Well, she left the Lennox place and went to the hotel. I waited around and after she went out I got a passkey, and . . ."

"But what about the murder weapon?"

"I'm coming to that," Larkin said. "I found a blouse with some bloodstains on it in her suitcase and Doc Carson made a test for me and said they were human bloodstains."

"Did you get a type?" Selby asked.

"Yes, he was able to give me a type—Type A."

"Just what made you feel that a woman stabbing another woman would get bloodstains on the front of her blouse?" Selby asked.

"Well, now," Larkin said, fidgeting, "I was working pretty fast there, fellows. I didn't have a chance to go into all the angles on this thing the way you would before a trial."

"Well, get to the murder weapon," Brandon said.

Larkin said hastily, "I found these bloodstains on the blouse. Now you take in a case of stabbing—well, it was a highly significant clue."

"You felt that it was blood from the victim?" Selby asked.

"Sure," Larkin said.

"And just how would Dorothy Clifton have got blood on the *front* of her blouse from stabbing another woman in the *back* when the evidence shows there was no spurting blood from the wound?"

"Well, she could have tripped and fallen, and fallen right on top of the body, or when she pulled the knife out she could have—well, anyway, it was blood, and I considered that a highly suspicious circumstance."

"Blood of Type A," Selby said. "Incidentally, the victim in this case had blood of Type O."

Larkin looked at him with the dazed expression of one who is trying to assimilate the importance of information but fails entirely to grasp its significance.

"The hell she did," he blurted.

"However, go ahead," Brandon said. "Let's get to this business of the murder weapon."

"Well," Larkin said, "when I found the bloodstained blouse and looked over the front seat of the automobile and found a little speck of blood on the side of the left-hand door—and all of this other stuff certainly fitted together, I went back out to the Lennox place and found out just where Dorothy Clifton's car had been parked. Then I started an intensive search."

Larkin was on more sure ground now, and it was impossible for him to keep a certain triumphant note from his voice.

"There's a driveway running along the side of the building into a double garage. There's a little portico effect on one side so you can step out of a car and be under cover as soon as you step out, and on the other side is a hedge. I combed that ground over pretty carefully. At first I didn't find anything, but I just kept moving along studying every inch of ground under the hedge."

Larkin paused dramatically, then said, "I found the murder weapon sticking with its point in the ground, just where somebody had thrown it. Just like you'd throw a dart."

"Where is it now?" Brandon asked.

Larkin said, "Doc Carson has it. He's going over it for bloodstains, and he's found some. It had been all wiped off slick and clean, but nevertheless there are bloodstains left on it."

"How about fingerprints?"

"No fingerprints. It had been wiped, really polished, but Doc Carson has some new test for finding bloodstains that's so sensitive you can bring them out on steel or on the handle of a knife even after it's been wiped off.

"Now, this murder weapon is a long thin stiletto with a horn handle; that is, it's made out of rings of horn strung on a thin piece of metal and then buffed off, the way they make those things down in Mexico, and there's a little etching on the blade that says, 'Tijuana, Mexico.'"

"You took photographs, of course, showing the position of the stiletto in the ground and marked exactly where you'd found it?"

Larkin ran his perspiring hand over his partially bald head, smoothing back the thin locks of hair. "It was pretty dark to take a photograph in there," he said. "It was right in under the hedge—and I was anxious to test the blade for fingerprints. I felt certain I'd find something on the blade or the handle and . . ."

"In other words, you didn't take photographs?"

"No."

"Did you mark the exact place?"

"Well, I can tell you right where it was, and . . ."

"Did you mark it?"

"No, I didn't mark it."

Selby said, "You know what's going to happen in this case, Larkin. You're going to be the key witness on finding that murder weapon. You're going to have to point out exactly where it was found and then you're going to have to stand up to cross-examination as to whether it was ten feet this way or ten feet that way."

"I can stand up. They can't rattle me."

"Or a foot this way or a foot that way."

"Well, of course," Larkin said, "when you get down to measurements like that it's a little difficult."

"Well, go ahead, where was it? Just how was it found?"

"Well, it was about halfway between the street and the portico, the blade sticking in the ground, just the way it would have been if someone driving up in an automobile had popped that dagger out of the automobile window."

"Dorothy Clifton's car was parked in front of the portico?"

"That's the way I understand it."

"And this dagger, then, was found *back* of where her car had been parked?"

"Where she'd popped it out of the window just as she was driving in," Larkin said positively.

"Popped it out of what window?" Selby asked.

"Why, the window on the side of the hedge."

"The right-hand side of the car?"

"That's right."

"Sticking in the ground at what angle?"

"Well, sort of slanting backwards."

"What do you mean by backwards?"

"Toward the street."

"You don't know the exact angle?"

"Well, sort of like this," Larkin said, holding up his finger.

Brandon studied the angle of the finger. Larkin, looking at it, slowly changed it a little, saying, "Well, perhaps a little more like this."

"Inclined toward the driveway or away from the driveway?" Selby asked.

"Well, I didn't notice that so much. I was looking to get the other angle. It was just about like this," Larkin announced, holding up his finger once more. "Just the way it would have been if someone had popped it in the ground, throwing it just like you would throw a dart."

"From the *right*-hand window of an automobile," Selby said.

"That's it."

"Then the angle must have been inclined rather sharply toward the driveway."

"No, it was sort of straight up and down."

"Just how could a person behind the steering wheel, on the left-hand side of a car, 'pop' a stiletto out of the right-hand window in the manner you have described," Selby asked, "without having the stiletto slanted sharply toward the car?"

"It must have hit a twig or something in the hedge and sort of straightened out," Larkin said."

"And it's the murder weapon?" Brandon asked.

"Doc Carson thinks it is. He performed the postmortem, you know, and he said the dagger just about fits the wound in the body. Now, the way I figure it, we can start work down in Tijuana and find out where these stilettos are sold and get a description of people who have bought them and probably get a photograph of this Dorothy Clifton and find somebody that will identify it. That way we can bring the murder weapon home to her, and then the case is an absolute cinch. There isn't any lawyer on earth that could upset it."

"And suppose we *can't* find someone who will remember having sold the weapon to Dorothy Clifton?" Selby asked.

"Well," Larkin said, "of course I'm not a lawyer, and I'm not the one who would be trying the case, but it looks to me like you've got a perfect case there, absolutely dead open-and-shut."

Selby said, "You'd better make a sketch of the exact position of that stiletto just as you found it. Make it while the facts are fresh in your mind."

He handed Larkin a piece of paper and a pencil.

Larkin made a crude diagram.

"Now, take it from the other side," Selby said. "Show the angle at which it was in the ground, looking at it parallel with the driveway."

Larkin said, "I think it was slanting toward the house all right. Just like it would have been if someone had popped it out of a car window."

"You didn't remember that a moment ago when we asked you," Brandon said.

"Well, I'm remembering it now," Larkin told him. "It was slanted just like it had been popped out of the right-hand window of an automobile."

"All right," Selby said wearily. "Just sign your name on the sketches, and write the date and time on them."

Larkin scrawled his signature and the date, pushed back his chair with evident eagerness, and said, "Well, I guess that's all the damage I can do here."

"Seems to be your usual quota," Brandon said dryly.

17

IT WAS SHORTLY BEFORE NOON WHEN KNUCKLES TAPPED on the door of the sheriff's private office.

"May I come in?" Sylvia Martin called.

"Come on in," Brandon invited. "Doug is the only one in here."

When she had opened the door, Selby said, "That was *some* story, Sylvia—the one about the meeting between Horace Lennox and Dorothy Clifton. Congratulations."

She said, "Thanks, Doug. Only I can't take any credit. The story wrote itself. I just sat back and fed paper into the typewriter. Oh, Doug, you should have seen it! I never saw anything so romantic in my life."

"I gathered as much from reading your account in *The Clarion* this morning."

"The way he took her in his arms! It makes you realize the solemnity of what it means when they say 'forsaking all others.' Doug, he's splendid! He's marvelous. He—oh, you can't begin to describe it. You could see that she had been having a question gnawing at the back of her consciousness. She knew how much he cared for his family, and how clannish they were, and how much they made a fetish of respectability and all that stuff, and here she was all mixed up in a murder case, and—well, you know, you could see that while she'd been in jail she hadn't been sleeping—just staring into the dark and wondering whether he'd stick with his family and be a little standoffish. You could see all of that question in her eyes."

"And then?" Brandon asked.

"You should have seen the way he answered that question!"

"What did he say?"

"Not what he said. It was what he did, and the way he did it. The question was never put into words and neither was the answer.

"All he said was *'Darling'* in a voice that was all choked up, and his arms went around her in the most tenderly reassuring way. It made me just stand there and cry. I kept saying to myself, 'Sylvia, you big goose. You're a newspaper woman'—but all the time I was writing up that story against a deadline I felt the tears pushing their way to the surface."

"It was a great story," Brandon said. "Made you feel all warm inside. A darned good antidote for the stuff that *The Blade* has been doing and the machinations of old A. B. Carr."

"What has Carr been doing?" she asked, instantly alert.

Selby said, "At a late hour last night, Frank Grannis was released on bail. It was a surety bond, purchased for him by an 'Old Friend,' whom I'll gamble he'd never seen before in all his life."

Sylvia said, "I can tell you something else. *The Blade* is organizing a citizens' committee. Of course, you can't pin it right on *The Blade,* but it's being done by people who are controlled by *The Blade.* They're calling what they refer to as a 'mass meeting' at the City Hall at two o'clock this afternoon, demanding that the attorney general appoint a special prosecutor to prosecute Dorothy Clifton. Of course, people who have any sense will ignore the whole thing. But the crackpots and *The Blade* henchmen will be there. They'll pass resolutions with a barb in them, indicating that you are completely hypnotized, under the domination and seductive influence of this murderess, and . . . oh, you know, it will make a great headline in *The Blade* tonight. I can just see it, MASS MEETING OF CITIZENS DEMANDS INCOMPETENT OR UNWILLING DISTRICT ATTORNEY WITHDRAW FROM CASE."

Selby said, "Why let them pull a stunt like that, Rex? Why shouldn't I go down?"

Brandon shook his head. "They won't be open-minded, Doug. They'll be soreheads whipped into line by *The Blade*. The thing will be stacked against you."

The telephone rang. Brandon picked it up, said, "Hello, yes? . . . What's that? . . . What's *that?*"

He said, "Hold the phone a minute. . . . Wait a minute, just tell me that all over again. . . . And you say he won't talk? . . . Okay. Hold the phone a minute."

Brandon placed his hand over the mouthpiece of the telephone and turned to Doug Selby. "Now, here's something. Grannis is back in jail at El Centro."

"What happened?"

"No one knows. The surety company that issued the bond produced him and said it desired to be relieved of liability."

Selby said, "Come on, Rex, we're driving to El Centro. Want to go, Sylvia?"

Sylvia shook her head. "I'm going to stay here, Doug. I'm going to take on the job of seeing that some of *your*

163

friends are at that 'mass' meeting, and then I'm going to see that one other person goes."

"Who?" Selby asked.

"Horace Lennox," she said, smiling. "*The Blade* saw to it that this meeting was held at such a time that they could come out with headlines telling about the action taken by the irate citizens, but by the time we get done with that meeting they may not *want* to publish what happened."

18

THE SHERIFF AT EL CENTRO WELCOMED BRANDON AND Selby and said, "There's certainly something screwy here. We thought this fellow Grannis was just a little simple, but it could be that he's pulling a fast one."

"How come?" Selby asked.

"This fellow who showed up to bail him out—darned if I don't think he was a complete stranger to Grannis, but they went through an act of being long-lost brothers.

"When I brought Grannis in I had a couple of other prisoners with him and this man who came to bail him out looked the three of them over, and looked blank as a sheet of paper. It was a development he hadn't expected, having three of them.

"Well, I was asleep at the switch and I didn't get the play for a minute, and I said, 'This man wants to see you, Grannis.' With that Grannis let out a war whoop and yelled, 'Hi, buddy!' and this guy ran forward and said, 'Frank, what the devil are they trying to do to you?' They patted each other on the back and shook hands, and you'd have thought it was a real family reunion. But there was a spell there, maybe four or five seconds, when they both just looked at each other without so much as a flicker of expression."

"You get this guy's name?" Brandon asked.

"Oh sure. I got his name and address and all the rest of it. He's a chap named Randles who's in the real estate business in Fallhaven. He's supposed to have been in the service with Grannis."

"What happened after that?" Brandon asked.

"Well, the bail bond was all in order and Randles took him away. Then first thing this morning, Randles was back saying there had been some trouble with the bonding company. Apparently the securities that he put up to guarantee the bonding company against loss weren't quite what the bonding company thought they should be or something, and the bonding company wanted to get out of its bond. So Randles surrendered Grannis, but said he was going out and get another surety bond, that he'd have Grannis out within twelve hours. He hasn't showed up since."

"Let's take a look at Grannis," Brandon said.

"I've got him here in the visitors' room waiting for you. Now, he knows you, Sheriff. You picked him up when he was first arrested. I didn't tell him who was coming, though. I just thought you boys could do your own talking."

"That's fine," Brandon said. "We'll see what he has to say."

The Imperial County sheriff led the way down a corridor, opened a door, and said, "Couple of boys to see you, Frank."

A young man sprang up from behind the table where he had been sitting, his face alert and eager. Then as he saw Brandon he promptly lost his smile and turned a glum countenance to Selby.

"Okay," he said, "what is it?"

Frank Grannis was about twenty-four, with dark,

slick hair, gray eyes spaced wide apart, and high cheekbones. There was a fullness to his lips which gave him the appearance of pouting. A slightly surly tilt to his mouth spoiled an otherwise intelligent and handsome face.

Sheriff Brandon said, "Frank, this is Doug Selby, the district attorney up in our county. He wants to ask you some questions."

"I don't think I want to talk with anyone."

"Well, that's all right," Selby said. "That's your privilege, you don't have to. I understood someone put up bail for you."

"That's right."

"And then surrendered you back into custody again."

"Yes."

"Do you know why?"

The prisoner's eyes avoided those of Selby. "No."

"This man Randles who put up the bail. He's an old friend of yours?"

"He's a friend."

"Known him long?"

"I don't see what that has to do with it."

"He put up money for your bail."

"He got a surety company to do it."

"And then something happened?"

"I believe so."

"Anyway, the surety company quit cold?"

"I believe so. They wanted to be relieved on their bond."

"What time were you let out of here?"

"The sheriff knows."

"Late last night?"

"Last night, yes."

167

"And where did you spend the night?"

"In a motel."

"Where?"

"I don't know the place. I'm a stranger here."

"Near here?"

"Not too near."

"Far?"

"Not so very far."

"You don't know where it was?"

"No."

"How long did it take you to get there?"

"I don't know for sure. We stopped and had some-thing to eat and, well, I just didn't keep track of the time."

"Did you get to the motel before midnight?"

"I don't know. I didn't look at my watch."

"Did you meet anyone there?"

"I saw someone there, yes."

"Who?"

"My lawyer."

"Anyone else?"

"What difference does it make?"

"And you stayed there in this motel?"

"I didn't get out and walk the streets."

"And then you were driven back here this morning?"

"Something was wrong with the bail bond. I don't know what."

"Who told you that?"

"I heard about it."

"Who told you?"

"I don't see as that makes any difference."

"Well, now how did you find out there was something wrong with the bail?"

"My lawyer told me."

"And how did he find out?"

"I don't know. I can't ask him all those things. He's a busy man."

"He certainly seems to be. Now that lawyer was Mr. A. B. Carr?"

"That's right. That's his name."

"Did it strike you as strange that a bail bond would be issued and then canceled right away?"

"Well, I was disappointed. I wanted to get out of this place and stay out, but that's the way it was."

"Well, what did you think?"

"I don't think. I'm not supposed to. I've got a lawyer who's paid to do the thinking."

"You're paying him?"

"If he wasn't being paid, he wouldn't bother with me, would he?"

"Now, Frank, I'm going to ask you something about that accident. You don't need to answer if you don't want to, but I want to get that thing straight in my own mind."

"I never had anything to do with that accident. I simply didn't hit that man."

"But a piece of the headlight from your automobile was found at the scene of the accident."

"That's what they tell me. But I'm certain my headlight was working properly when I drove in to that motel at Madison City."

"And the glass was in the headlight?"

"Well, I'm not entirely certain about the glass. I know my headlights showed the road all right. I was so tired I could hardly keep my eyes open. I'd had a long drive and I was all in. I just tumbled out of the car and into bed."

"Was someone riding with you?"

"You know someone was."

"Who?"

"A girl from Montana. Daphne Arcola her name is. I picked her up at the checking station at Yuma."

"You know her name now. Yet you didn't know it a few days ago."

"I read it in the paper last night. My friend had a copy of *The Blade* with him—that's how he knew where I was and that I was being held on a hit-and-run charge.

"And that's how I knew who this girl was. At the time I gave her the ride I only knew her first name, and I'd even forgotten that.

"She didn't want to talk much, and I was dog tired. I'd been driving all day and then I picked her up. She was a nice kid and she was very anxious to get to Los Angeles.

"Ordinarily I'd have turned in at Brawley, but she was so anxious to get in to Los Angeles I thought I'd try to make it on through if I possibly could. I hated to think of a nice kid like that being loose on the highway, having to hitchhike. I was so sleepy I was blacking out, but I tried to keep going."

"Don't you suppose you could have blacked out and hit this man?"

"No. I wasn't blacking out that bad. And anyway she was there wide awake."

"Why didn't you let her drive?"

"Just because . . . well, when you pick up someone you're foolish to let them drive. It's too easy for them to conk you and take the car. She looked like a sweet kid, but there was something strange about the way she . . . I guess, Mr. Selby, I don't want to do any more talking about that case. I don't think I should."

"Let's go back to last night, then. You stayed in a motel?"

"That's right."

"And what sort of a place was it? A pretty good place?"

"High-class."

"And Randles stayed there with you?"

"I didn't say he did."

"But he took you there?"

"Yes."

"And came and got you this morning and took you back?"

"That's when it turned out there was something wrong with the bail. He had to protect himself. You can't blame him for that."

"Certainly not," Selby said. "What's he doing about that, anything?"

"He's fixing it up. I'm going to get out on bail pretty soon."

"How soon?"

"Almost any time now."

Selby said, "Perhaps if you could get this Daphne Arcola to go to the district attorney here and explain that you didn't hit anyone, he might dismiss the case against you."

"I don't think so. He's an old grouch. He says I'm trying to pull some sort of a runaround. He's sitting tight about that piece of broken headlight. I tell you, I think someone framed me on that."

"How?"

"I don't know how, but I didn't hit anyone. I'm certain I didn't."

"Look here," Brandon said, "we know that you and Carr had a talk last night and laid some plans for your defense. Now who else was there?"

"You see my lawyer," Grannis said, "and that's all I'm going to say. I've talked too much already."

Selby got to his feet. "All right, if that's the way you feel about it, Frank. I thought perhaps we could help you."

"Sure," Grannis said, "I know the way *you* want to help." He raised his chin and drew his extended forefinger across his throat.

"All right, if that's the way you want to have it," Selby said. "Come on, Rex, let's go."

They left the visitors' room. The El Centro sheriff, waiting for them, asked, "Did you get anything out of him?"

"Something," Selby said, "but I don't know just what. I don't know just what the significance of it is."

"Boy, that lawyer of his is a smooth one. How do you suppose a guy with no more money than he has managed to get a high-powered lawyer like that?"

"Darned if I know," Selby said, "but he certainly seems to have a high-powered lawyer."

"You can say that again."

"Well," Brandon asked as they left the jail, "what do you make of Grannis?"

"The kid hates to lie," Selby said. "He can hardly look us in the eye when he's talking about what happened last night. And, because he hates to lie, he's trying to tell the truth as far as he can and then resort to lies when he has to."

"You don't believe all of that stuff about the bond, do you?"

"No."

"Neither do I. I'm telling you, Doug, there's something funny about that. They got him out for some particular purpose. They were taking a risk on getting him out and they knew it. They didn't intend to risk their money any longer than was necessary. They had to have him out for some particular purpose and they put up the bail money and got him out. Then, as soon as they'd accomplished that purpose, they put him back in."

Selby said, "Well, you can gamble one thing. Frank Grannis, a stranger in California, didn't pick A. B. Carr as the man to represent him simply by some form of telepathic communication. He got the best criminal lawyer in the country and *that* wasn't accident."

"What do *you* think it was?" Brandon asked.

Selby said, "I don't think it was money. I don't think Grannis has that sort of money. There's nothing to indicate it."

"Go ahead, son," Brandon said, "you're doing fine. Keep right on talking."

"Therefore," Selby said, "Carr is going to do something for Grannis, and Grannis must be going to do something for Carr."

"Perhaps be a witness?"

Selby nodded.

"But," Brandon said, "it's the other way around, Doug. Carr is the one who is digging up the witness."

"And that," Selby said, "is the part that simply doesn't make sense. Grannis should be doing something to help Carr in return for Carr's legal services. In place of that,

173

Carr seems to be acting purely in the interests of justice and with no thought of compensation—and you know that's not right."

Brandon opened the door of the big county sedan, slid in behind the steering wheel. Doug Selby got in from the other side. Brandon backed out of the parking place, said, "Well, we keep running around in circles every time we try to follow old A. B. C.'s back tracks."

"Wait a minute," Selby said suddenly. "I wonder if I haven't got something after all, Rex."

"What?" Brandon asked.

Selby said, "Remember when we met Horace Lennox at the office last night?"

"Uh-huh."

Selby said excitedly, "Remember we talked with him about Dorothy Clifton and he said he was going to stay by her, and we asked him if he'd seen the family and he said he'd talked with his mother and Steve?"

"Uh-huh."

"But," Selby said, "he didn't say he talked with Moana."

"Well, he must have talked with her," Brandon said. "She was probably even more bitter than his mother. She's in a position . . . say, wait a minute."

"Exactly," Selby said. "The reason he didn't talk with Moana is because she wasn't there. And A. B. Carr was somewhere, and Frank Grannis was somewhere. And whenever we'd start crowding Frank Grannis on where he was, and who else besides his lawyer was with him, he'd shift his eyes and get evasive."

"But what in the world would he have been doing meeting Moana Lennox?"

"That," Selby said, "could be the pay-off, Rex."

"What do you mean?"

"Grannis couldn't pay Carr enough money to compensate old A. B. C. for representing him. But perhaps he could do something for old A. B. C. that would help Carr make money from another client."

"But why should Moana be . . . gosh, Doug, you don't think *she* could have . . ." Brandon let the sentence remain unfinished.

Selby said, "I don't want to jump at conclusions, Rex, but something important happened last night and Grannis talked with someone whom he doesn't dare mention. . . . Let's just start checking up on where certain people were last night."

Brandon grinned, pushed his foot down on the throttle. "*Now* we're getting somewhere, Doug. It sounds like a darn good theory."

"It isn't a theory," Selby said, "only a hunch."

"Far as I can see it's a darn good hunch, Doug. I bet it pays off."

Selby said, "It's the way Carr would do the thing."

"Wish we could beat him at his own game," Brandon said. "Wouldn't we be justified in using fire to fight the devil with, Doug?"

Selby shook his head. "Our hands are tied, Rex. As representatives of the law we have only two weapons we can use—brains and two-fisted honesty."

"Honesty can't stand up to the sort of ingenious trickery old A. B. C. uses," Rex Brandon said bitterly. "He thinks nothing of bribery and . . ."

"I said *Two-Fisted Honesty*," Selby reminded the sheriff.

Brandon thought that over for a moment, then grinned. "I gottcha now, Doug."

175

19

HORACE LENNOX, HIS FACE DRAWN, AND WITH DEEPLY etched lines at the corners of his mouth, entered the sheriff's office, and said, "You sent for me, sir?"

"Yes, Horace. Doug Selby and I want to talk with you for a minute."

"Yes, sir. What about?"

"It's about your sister, Moana."

Horace raised his eyebrows.

"You've decided to stand up for Dorothy Clifton on this thing?"

"Naturally."

Brandon said, in a kindly voice, "Horace, it gets back to what happened the night this girl was murdered. Dorothy says that someone took her car."

Horace nodded.

"I'm afraid your mother thinks that's merely something Dorothy made up," Selby said.

"I'm afraid so."

"But you know, and I know that *someone* must have taken her car."

Horace nodded.

"Could it have been Moana?"

"I don't think so."

"Why?"

"I don't know. Moana's secretive. She likes to play

'em close to her chest, but she wouldn't have done a thing like that. If she'd taken the car, she'd have come forward and said so."

"Did you see her when you got home last night?"

"No."

"But you have talked with her?" Brandon asked, glancing significantly at Selby.

"Yes."

"When?"

"About an hour ago."

"Where was she when you arrived home last night? Asleep?"

"She wasn't home. She'd gone up to see her closest friend who lives at Santa Barbara. Poor kid. I guess she was pretty much upset with all the publicity, and so forth. The Lennox clan isn't accustomed to—well, to seeing its name in the paper, particularly in this connection."

"So she went up to see her friend?"

"Yes."

"Who is this friend?"

"Mrs. Jordon L. Kerry, Connie—short for Constance. She and Moana were inseparable before Connie married."

"You talked with Moana after she came home?"

"Yes. She's a good kid. She likes Dorothy. I think she's pretty thoroughly convinced that no matter what else happened, Dorothy must be innocent. But what with the loss of that jewelry and the shock of having someone break into the house and all that—well, the kid's pretty much upset."

"And you don't think *she* took Dorothy's car?"

"I don't think she took the car. But I *do* think it could

177

have been one of the servants. I'm not eliminating them from the picture until I've done a lot more investigating. And then there's—there's one other possibility."

"What's that?"

Horace hesitated, then shook his head. "I don't think I care to discuss it."

Brandon looked at Selby, then started drumming on the desk. "Okay, Horace," he said at length. "Thanks a lot for your help. I was just trying to check up on things."

"What's happening with—with the case?"

"Oh, lots of developments," Brandon said. "Nothing that's really determinative, but we're keeping after it."

"You'll let me know?" Horace asked with sharp anxiety in his voice.

"Sure, sure," Brandon said reassuringly.

When Horace had left, Brandon pulled the telephone book toward him, started looking down the list, then said, "Here's the number at Santa Barbara. Let's call."

He put in a person-to-person call. "The sheriff's office," he said, "I want to talk with Mrs. Jordon L. Kerry at Santa Barbara. Rush the call through, will you? It's something of an emergency."

He held on to the phone, then after a few moments said, "Hello . . . yes, hello. Mrs. Kerry? This is Sheriff Brandon speaking. You're very friendly with Moana Lennox and I'm trying to check up on some jewelry she has. Would you know the jewelry if you saw it again? . . . I see, you would. . . . When did you see Moana last, Mrs. Kerry? . . . Oh yes. . . . What time? . . . I see. . . . All right, thank you. I was just trying to check up on that jewelry. We don't have too good a description. We may be on the trail of something. I

178

think we *may* be able to find the burglar, and if we do we're going to require an ironclad identification. As a matter of fact, we're on a hot trail right now. . . . Well, thanks a lot."

He hung up, said, "Moana was up there last night all right. She drove up and she and Constance talked almost all night. Mrs. Kerry says she was in quite a state of nerves and seems all broken up about the fact that Dorothy is suspected of the murder. She says it will ruin her brother's life, and the girl is on the verge of hysterics."

Selby puffed thoughtfully on his pipe. "Of course, Rex," he said, "with all of the emotional problems that are confronting her, it's only natural that she'd like to go and see her best friend, but—hang it, Rex, somehow I can't help wondering if there isn't something more to it than that."

"Oh, I suppose so," Brandon said, wearily, "but the point is she wasn't with old A. B. Carr and Frank Grannis, so there's nothing in that lead."

"Hang it," Selby said. "I suppose I'm getting jumpy. Every move we make we run up against old A. B. Carr, and I suppose my perspective is becoming warped, but . . . Rex, *do* you suppose there's a possibility Moana wasn't up there; that this is an alibi that's been cooked up by Carr?"

"Why would *she* want an alibi?"

"I don't know," Selby said, and for several moments gave himself up to thoughtful contemplation as he puffed slowly at his pipe.

"I feel that jewel burglary was an inside job, Rex."

"So do I."

"I don't think it could have happened exactly the

way Moana described it. Now then, whom would Moana be protecting?"

The sheriff said, "You're getting into deep water there, Doug. The Lennox family is firmly entrenched in this town, and any time we start opening their closet doors looking for skeletons, we're going to have to know which closet and what skeleton."

Selby said, "If Moana is up to anything—if there is any connection between her and old A. B. C., she'll have been warned against betraying herself by any unconscious slip."

Once more Selby sought solace in his pipe, then suddenly he said, "Rex, suppose we could get her away from her family. Get her up here in the office under such circumstances that she thought she was here for another purpose, and then suddenly start grilling her on where she was last night."

Brandon said, "It would have to be done very cleverly, Doug, and you couldn't afford to let her know you were doubting her word about anything until you were certain you had the goods on her. The family has lots of friends and *The Blade* would like nothing better than to claim we were trying to dig up a red herring to compensate for having lost out to Otto Larkin on a solution of the case."

Selby said, "We're on a spot, Rex. Everyone will expect us to go ahead and prosecute Dorothy Clifton for murder, but there isn't one scrap of evidence connecting the murder weapon with her. Anyone could have gone out and planted that murder weapon in the hedge *after* knowing that Dorothy Clifton had been questioned. I don't think Dorothy Clifton's guilty, and I don't want to prosecute her."

"The only way we can get out of prosecuting her is to find the person who did do it," Brandon pointed out.

"Let's assume that burglary was an inside job, Rex. Who did it?"

"Dorothy Clifton might have," Brandon said. "About one chance in a million. Mrs. Lennox might have had some reason for doing it. Then when Moana wakened she could have hurried out of the room, up the back stairs, and into the upper corridor, and down the front stairs."

Selby nodded.

"But," Brandon went on, "the most logical suspect is Steve. Steve may have found himself trapped in some predicament, something that a youngster gets into. He had to have money fast. And then, of course, there's one other possibility."

"What's that?"

"Moana could be protecting herself—but we need evidence, Doug. We can't play hunches in a matter of that kind."

Selby cupped the warm bowl of his pipe in his hand. "Rex, suppose we should recover that stolen jewelry."

"That, of course, would be the answer," Brandon said.

"And if Moana were protecting anyone, when she knew that we'd recovered the jewelry, she'd blurt out the whole story."

"If we'd recovered the jewelry, she wouldn't need to blurt out anything," Brandon said.

"But suppose she *thought* we'd recovered the jewelry. Then she'd tell her story, wouldn't she?"

"Probably."

"You have sketches of the jewelry, Rex?"

The sheriff nodded.

"Stacy Bodega, of the Bodega Jewelry Company, has a large collection of antique jewelry. He's not only a collector, but a speculator. He thinks the market is going up on it later on and he's saving all he can get his hands on. He's almost certain to have some jewelry that almost duplicates the jewelry taken from Moana's dresser drawer.

"Suppose we get in touch with him, show him the sketches of the stolen jewelry, then get Moana in here, and tell her that we've recovered her jewelry. Let her just get a glimpse of it at the start. Don't give her a chance to make a careful comparison for identification, but with all the assurance in the world tell her we've recovered the jewelry and then look at her accusingly. She should break down and give us some information."

"It's worth trying," Brandon said. "In fact, at this stage of the game almost anything is worth trying."

Selby reached over and picked up the sheriff's telephone, said to the operator, "Get the Lennox residence. I want to talk with Miss Moana Lennox. Tell her it's the district attorney calling."

He held the phone a moment, then heard Mrs. Lennox saying very firmly, "I'm sorry, but the child simply cannot be disturbed. This is her mother and . . ."

"I'll talk with her," Selby cut in. Then in his most suave tone said, "Hello, Mrs. Lennox. This is Mr. Selby, the district attorney. We're working on a very important clue. I'm going to have some jewelry here in about an hour that I want Moana to look at. I have reason for wanting to keep the matter *very* confidential. Will you please have Moana come to the sheriff's office in about an hour?"

"Couldn't you bring it out here?"

"Under the circumstances," Selby said, mysteriously, "circumstances which I am not at liberty to explain, that would be very inconvenient. I'd like very much to have Moana come to the sheriff's office."

"In an hour?" Mrs. Lennox inquired.

"In an hour," Selby said. "And please have her come alone and without letting anyone know where she's going."

"Very well, Mr. Selby, and thank you for your efforts. However, Mr. Selby, I certainly hope that you're not going to let that creature pull the wool over your eyes."

"That creature?"

"That Dorothy Clifton person. She has completely hypnotized my son, Horace. I am very much pained to see that he is so credulous. I have spent a great deal of money giving him a legal education, and I certainly think that an attorney should be a little less naïve. Particularly so far as designing females are concerned. I certainly hope, Mr. Selby, that *you're* not going to be taken in by this creature's wiles. If the jewelry you have is Moana's, it came from Dorothy Clifton. If it didn't come from her, then it isn't Moana's jewelry.

"This creature is not only responsible for all of our troubles, but I'm certain that she's the one who entered Moana's bedroom and stole that jewelry. We had been talking about Moana's jewelry that night before Dorothy went to bed. She must have committed the murder and then taken Moana's jewelry. When the case is finally solved that will be definitely and positively established. In fact, I shall insist that it is definitely and positively established so that my son can come to his senses."

"Thank you, Mrs. Lennox," Selby said. "In about an hour then."

"In an hour," she said, and hung up.

Selby turned to the sheriff with a grin. "Well," he said, "we're starting to burn bridges, Rex. Let me have those sketches of the stolen jewelry. I'm going to see Stacy Bodega, dig up some earrings, a brooch, and a pendant."

Brandon looked at his watch. "It's two now. She'll be in here at three o'clock then."

Selby nodded. "Don't worry, I'll be here in time with the jewelry. I'm certain Stacy Bodega will co-operate."

20

SELBY SPREAD THE ANTIQUE JEWELRY OUT ON SHERIFF
Brandon's desk, glanced at his watch, and said, "Well, I
have a few minutes to spare. I hope she'll be prompt."

"That stuff certainly matches the sketches," Brandon
said. "Gosh, Doug, you don't suppose that by any chance
it could be the same stuff, do you?"

"Not the same stuff, Rex, but it could be *almost* the
same. Jewelry of that particular period all followed a
certain fixed pattern. This is close enough to it to give
us something to work on. We can say that . . ."

Selby broke off as the door of the sheriff's office opened
and Sylvia Martin entered the room.

"May I interrupt long enough to see if there's any new
lead?" she asked.

Selby nodded, said, "There isn't anything definite yet,
Sylvia, but I have a good human-interest story for you,
if you want to go to Santa Barbara."

"What is it?"

"Moana Lennox's closest girl friend lives up there.
She's married now, Mrs. Jordon L. Kerry. Moana apparently went up there last night. She's all worked up
about the things that are happening, and about her
brother's broken romance."

"I don't see anything broken about it," Sylvia said.

"It isn't, but Moana thought it would be. She naturally couldn't conceive of a Lennox turning against the sacred Lennox family."

"No, I suppose not. . . . What have you there, Doug? Don't tell me that's the jewelry that. . . ."

"We won't tell you it is, but we won't tell you what it . . ." He broke off as the door opened and A. B. Carr, accompanied by Phillip L. Paden, entered the room.

"Good afternoon, gentlemen," Carr said, in his richly resonant voice, "and pardon me. My dear Miss Martin, I trust that you're acquainted with the new publisher of your competitive sheet. If not, permit me to present Mr. Phillip L. Paden. Miss Martin, Mr. Paden."

"I've met him," Sylvia said shortly.

Brandon casually moved away from the desk and jewelry. "What is it you fellows want?"

"I think," Carr said, "that the jewelry over there is the thing which primarily interests us, Sheriff. Miss Moana Lennox asked me to take a look at some jewelry you had here. You see, among other things, Sheriff, I'm something of a connoisseur of antique jewelry. It's been a hobby of mine for some time and . . ."

"The devil it has!"

"Oh, yes. I've quite a collection of antique jewelry of my own, and it happens I was talking with Miss Lennox some months ago about antique jewelry generally. She told me she had some very interesting pieces which were heirlooms, and was good enough to show them to me. So I'm thoroughly familiar with them. I believe you thought these might be hers?"

Brandon said, "I don't think we care to discuss this jewelry with you, Carr."

"Why not?"

"There are certain confidential aspects of the case."

Carr walked over to examine the jewelry, said cheerfully, "Well, you won't need to discuss it, Sheriff, because I can tell you right now that this is not Moana Lennox's jewelry."

"It's not?"

"Definitely not. It's of the same period and similar design, but it's not the same jewelry."

Paden, smiling expansively, lit a cigar. "Do you recognize it at all, Carr? Ever seen it before?"

"Well, now," Carr said, hesitating, "I wouldn't want to express an absolute opinion. There's nothing that's more difficult than to make a positive identification in matters of this sort, but I *think* I've seen that jewelry before. I think it's part of a collection belonging—or which did belong to Mr. Stacy Bodega. He had it on exhibit about a year ago and I was very much interested in some of his pieces."

"Well," Paden said, *"that's* interesting. How about it, Sheriff? Where did you get it?"

Brandon said, "As far as *The Blade* is concerned, this office has ceased giving out any information whatever. If you want information, go out and get it."

"Okay," Paden said, "I will. And when I get it I'll know what to do with it. Don't think any two-bit hick sheriff is going to tell me where to get off. You're holding office, Brandon, until the next election, and that's the end of it, so there's no need to push your weight around. A year from now and you won't have any official weight to push around. Good day, sir."

Brandon followed him to the door. "The trouble with this community is it's getting too damn citified. First we get a shyster lawyer, and then we get a crooked publisher."

Paden said, "Those words are libelous and my attorney . . ." He turned, saw the look in Sheriff Brandon's eyes, hesitated a moment, then hurried out into the corridor.

Brandon, following him, said, "That's what I said. A crooked newspaper publisher, and a shyster lawyer."

"Come on, Paden," Carr said suavely. "*You* can answer him in the columns of your paper. *I* can afford to ignore it."

They walked rapidly toward the stairs.

Brandon kicked the door shut, his face white with fury. "Damn them," he said. "They haven't guts enough to turn around and make a fair fight of it. They keep sniping away in that dirty newspaper. Hang it, that man Carr! He *would* have to turn out to be a connoisseur of antique jewelry."

"Doug," Sylvia said, "*did* you get that from Bodega's collection?"

Selby nodded. "I was trying to lay a trap for Moana. I wanted to get her in here and—well, that's what happened. How in the world would anyone from the Lennox family ever get teamed up with A. B. Carr?"

Sylvia said, "Oh Doug, I'm afraid you walked right into a trap. Didn't you ever hear about Stacy Bodega's son? He was arrested for drunken driving while he was in college. He hit a woman and injured her quite seriously.

"Bodega got old A. B. C., and Carr fixed everything up very hush-hush. Now you can see what must have happened. Stacy Bodega must have been passing the time of day with Carr and undoubtedly mentioned that you'd gone over his collection to try and match the Lennox pieces."

Selby's face darkened. "And that's why Carr brought Paden along with him. . . . Still Carr must have had *some* connection with the Lennox family—with Moana, anyway. What do *you* say, Rex?"

Brandon said, "What I want to say can't be said in front of Sylvia. Damn them!"

Selby turned to a thoroughly miserable Sylvia Martin. "Here's a tip, Sylvia. Charter an airplane. Fly up to Santa Barbara and talk with Constance Kerry, and I mean *talk* with her. If there's anything fishy about this thing, and I think there is, I want you to find out about it. Telephone just as soon as you get a lead."

He walked to the door with her.

Suddenly she turned, drew his head over and kissed his cheek.

"Remember, Doug, there are thousands of people in this county who believe in you, who trust you—who love you."

He patted her shoulder.

"And now," she said, "wipe the lipstick off your cheek. Let's have at them."

"Hip and thigh," he agreed laughingly. "We'll smite them . . . Sylvia . . . ?"

"Yes."

"You said there were thousands who loved me?"

She nodded.

"That's more than I need, Sylvia. It's nine hundred and ninety-nine more than I need."

"You'll need every one before you're through with this case," she told him, and slipped quietly through the door into the corridor.

21

SELBY SAT IN REX BRANDON'S OFFICE. THE DOOR WAS locked. A copy of the evening *Blade*, still damp from the press, was spread out on Brandon's desk.

Brandon said, "That other stuff was vicious, Doug. This attack is really deadly. It's going to hurt. This is the stuff voters read, believe and fall for."

Headlines streamed across the front page: SHERIFF AND D. A. FAKE RECOVERY OF JEWELRY TO HIDE INEFFICIENCY."

Brandon skimmed through the news account, turned to the editorial page, said, "Listen to this, Doug. Here's the way Paden's fighting now:

In a last desperate attempt to conceal their failure and presumably to try and detract from the credit due Otto Larkin for apprehending the Number One murder suspect in connection with the killing of Rose Furman, Doug Selby, the district attorney, and Rex Brandon, the sheriff, have perpetrated what is probably the greatest comic opera scheme of them all.

It has now been definitely established that these men went to a collector of antique jewelry and borrowed some pieces which would answer the description of the jewelry which was taken from the Lennox home in a burglary last Tuesday night.

They next sent for their staunch ally on *The Clarion* to

be certain there would be plenty of favorable publicity, and then notified Moana Lennox that her jewelry had been recovered and asked her to come and identify it.

It happened that Moana Lennox, who had been prostrated by the shock of the burglary in addition to events indirectly connecting her family with the murder of Rose Furman, was unable to keep the appointment, but she knew that A. B. Carr, the distinguished lawyer who has seen fit to honor this city by making his home in our midst, was an expert on antique jewelry, an avid collector, and a shrewd appraiser.

It happened that Carr had seen Moana Lennox's heirlooms and so she asked him to drop by the sheriff's office and see if it would be possible to make an identification.

Not only did Carr fail to identify the jewelry as that of Moana Lennox, but to the discomfited surprise of the red-faced county officials, he made a positive identification of the jewelry as being a part of the collection of Stacy Bodega, the local jeweler who has for a long time made a hobby of collecting interesting bits of antique jewelry.

It was only the work of a few minutes to confirm the hoax which the officers had attempted to perpetrate in order to secure favorable publicity from a friendly newspaper. Stacy Bodega reluctantly admitted that the officials had borrowed this jewelry from him earlier in the day.

In the past, these officials have enjoyed the fawning support of a sycophant press, and favorable publicity has been lavished upon them in screaming headlines whenever they blundered upon any clues which automatically led to the solution of such crimes as they were investigating. One would have thought that these men were combinations of Sherlock Holmes and Solomon.

Then came the murder of Rose Furman, and the comedy of errors which resulted when the district attorney and the sheriff, starting out in their usual bungling way, attempted to muddle through.

Had the breaks been with them, it is probable that once more the subservient *Clarion* would have been screaming at the top of its vociferous lungs that the astute county officials once again had solved a murder which would have baffled any detectives other than those super-shrewd sleuths who are guarding over the destinies of Madison County.

As it was, Otto Larkin quietly, unostentatiously, and with no fanfare of trumpets, went out and solved that murder case. At least he has the prime Number One suspect in custody, and while it is not the policy of *The Blade* to attempt to try cases in the newspaper, or to anticipate what a jury may do, we will, nevertheless, state that the evidence which can be introduced, and which should be introduced by a special prosecutor appointed by the attorney general, will be damning.

Rex Brandon was probably a good cattleman. He should be back in the cattle business. There is some question as to whether Doug Selby possesses sufficient brains to make a living in private, competitive practice of law. Selby probably knows better than anyone else. And his own opinion is shown by his actions. Immediately on his return from the Army, he used the halo of his military service to plunge once more into the haven of a job where the taxpayers of this community would see that he enjoyed a fixed income.

It will be interesting to see what Doug Selby can actually do when he is retired to private life, because the chances that he will retain the office of the district attorney after the next election are figured by shrewd gamblers at about ten thousand to one.

Elsewhere in the news columns will be found the story of a meeting of the citizens for the purpose of petitioning the attorney general to send in a special prosecutor to relieve the unwilling and incompetent district attorney's office of the prosecution of Dorothy Clifton, who is at present under arrest awaiting trial for the murder of Rose Furman.

An attempt by Selby's sympathizers to stampede the

meeting resulted in a disorderly exhibition of name calling which finally broke up with no definite action taken. But the citizens are grimly determined to see that something is done, and another mass meeting will be called in the near future where Selby sympathizers will be so far outnumbered there will be no opportunity for "packing" the meeting.

Brandon pushed the paper back, looked up, and said, "People like to be on the side of the winner, Doug. As long as *The Blade* adopts the position that we're has-beens and also-rans, and can pour out that sort of propaganda, people are going to fall for it. *The Blade* will call another mass meeting within the next few days. They'll manage to stampede a lot of people into petitioning the attorney general to send in a special prosecutor to handle the case against Dorothy Clifton."

Selby nodded. "Of course that jewelry business backfired, Rex. I led with my chin. I wanted to get Moana where we could question her. I'm suspicious about that theft of the jewelry and . . . oh, well, the breaks went against me. I'm sorry I dragged you into it."

" 'Dragged me in' nothing," Brandon said. "I was with you hand-in-glove. I felt certain it would be a good idea. It . . ."

The telephone rang. Brandon picked up the receiver. "Hello, Brandon talking," then said, "Oh, hello. Yes, Sylvia. . . . Yes, he's right here. . . . Okay, I'll let you talk with him."

Sylvia Martin's voice came over the wire sharp with excitement. "Doug," she said, "there's something funny about this whole business. I went in to get an interview from Mrs. Kerry. She didn't want to see me. When I finally got to her, she wouldn't talk. I started intimating that I knew something, and believe me, Doug, she's scared to death. I don't know what it is, but she's absolutely frightened stiff. She says Moana comes to see her whenever she's upset. She insists that Moana was there last night and also spent the night with her a couple of months ago, but she's white-faced, and her husband is definitely against the whole thing. He said that as far as he was concerned he had nothing to say, and he was gruff about it. Doug, there's something, somewhere, that needs looking into in connection with this woman's story. She's covering up something."

"Where are you now?" Selby asked.

"I'm still up here."

"You've finished your interview?"

"It was finished for me. I was virtually thrown out on my ear."

"Okay. Come on back," Selby said. "I'm going to set off some fireworks and you may want to watch them."

Selby hung up and said to Rex Brandon, "Okay, Rex. The way things are now we're in just about as bad as we can get. Personally, I never won any battles remaining on the defensive."

"What are you going to do?" Brandon asked.

Selby said, "Let's look at it this way. Carr is mixed into this thing up one side and down the other. He's supposed to know all about Moana Lennox's jewelry because she showed it to him. All right, he knows about it. That means she showed it to him. How did it happen she showed it to him?"

"She knew he was interested in antique jewelry and . . ."

"Bunk!" Selby interrupted. "Carr's interested in antique jewelry. Carr's also interested in fees. Carr's primarily interested in power. The reason Moana Lennox *showed* that jewelry to Carr is because she wanted Carr to do something for her and she didn't have the money. So she turned the jewelry over to him and then, in order to account for its disappearance, cut the screen from the inside and, at what she considered was a propitious moment, started screaming."

Brandon thought that over. "It *could* be, all right," he said.

"Try to think of another explanation that covers the facts," Selby challenged.

Brandon gave the matter thought, then said, "It's a possibility, all right. But it's something we'd never be able to prove."

Selby said, "I'm tired of being on the defensive. I'm tired of sticking around here letting Carr snipe at me. I like him. I appreciate the man's intelligence. He's a genius. He's also a crook. I believe he has that jewelry."

"Wouldn't he have disposed of it?"

"He wouldn't dare to, because he must have known that Moana was going to claim it had been stolen. Therefore, if it should be located in a pawn shop, it could be traced back to him. As I see it, there's a darn good chance that Carr has that jewelry and is going to hold it until after everything has blown over so it'll be safe to dispose of it. That jewelry is Carr's fee."

"Gosh, if we could only prove something like that, Doug! But we can't do it."

"Why not?"

"A. B. C. would have covered his back trail. Moana would never talk. If we tried to reach her we'd run into a play just like we did when we . . ."

Selby got to his feet. "Okay, Rex. I'm going to break an egg."

"Do what, Doug?"

Selby grinned. "There's an old saying that you can't make an omelette without breaking eggs. I'm going to make an omelette."

"And the eggs you're breaking?" Brandon asked.

"I'm personally going to hunt up a justice of the peace and get a search warrant. After all, the jewelry is supposed to be stolen."

"Gosh, Doug, it's too risky. If it's a wrong guess we'd be liable for damages, and we'd be the laughingstock of . . ."

"Not *we*," Selby said. "This is one thing you're going to keep out of. I'm personally going to . . ."

Brandon pushed back his chair. "Who the hell do you think you're talking to? *I'm* personally going to serve that warrant."

22

LEFTY, THE BUTLER WITH THE CAULIFLOWER EAR, AN-
swered the door.

"Mr. Carr home?" Selby asked.

"No, sir, Mr. Carr is not at home."

"Mrs. Carr home?"

"No, sir, she's not at home."

Selby said, "This happens to be a matter of considerable importance. It's very much to Mr. Carr's interests
that he knows I'm here."

"He's not at home."

"All right," Brandon said, pushing forward. "You
see this? I suppose you know what this is?"

"What is it?"

"It's a search warrant," Selby said. "We're searching
this house for stolen property."

"You and who else?"

"I'm making the search," Brandon said truculently.

"You're not coming in here, warrant or no warrant."

"This is a warrant," Brandon said. "I'm the sheriff.
I'm serving it and I'm coming in. I don't know what
your record is, but if you want to add resisting an officer
to it that's fine. And if you want to back up your play
I'm going to start putting chips on the table. Now then,
stand to one side. I'm coming in."

The man blocked the door with his big body.

Brandon suddenly shoved his shoulder against the man's chest, pushed him back off balance.

Lefty, weaving from the hips after the manner of a professional pugilist, started for Brandon.

Brandon stood stock-still, but his browned right hand dropped to the weapon at his belt. He said, ominously and steely-eyed, "You're resisting an officer in the performance of his duties."

Lefty hesitated. The cold glitter of Brandon's eyes held him.

Brandon said, "I wouldn't use fists if I were you, Lefty. Either stand to one side or else start reaching for a gun if you've got one. This is a showdown. I'm playing with blue chips."

"I haven't got a gun," Lefty said hastily.

"I have," Brandon told him.

The butler seemed unable to remove his eyes from Brandon.

Suddenly there were steps in the corridor and Carr's voice said, "Dear me, what's all the commotion? Well, well! My good friends Selby and the sheriff! That's quite all right, Lefty. Let them in. I'm sorry, gentlemen, but I had left word that I wasn't to be disturbed under any circumstances. I was afraid that there might be an attempt on the part of the press to . . . But *do* come in."

"We're coming in," Brandon said. "This time I'm coming in not as a guest, but as an officer of the law. I have a search warrant for this place."

"A *search* warrant?" Carr exclaimed incredulously.

"A search warrant," Brandon said.

"For heaven's sake what . . . ?"

"I'll tell you in a very few words, Carr. I have a search

198

warrant authorizing me to search these premises for certain stolen jewelry."

"Stolen jewelry!" Carr exclaimed. "Stolen jewelry? Are you crazy? What would *I* want with stolen jewelry."

"I have a search warrant. I'm going to search."

"Good heavens, Selby," Carr said, *"you're* an attorney. You know that a warrant of that sort can't be issued unless there's an affidavit filed and a showing of probable cause."

"I've made the affidavit," Selby said.

"You have!"

"That's right, and the jewelry we're looking for is the antique jewelry with which, as it happens, you are so remarkably and fortuitously familiar. The jewelry which belonged to Moana Lennox."

Carr for once in his life seemed completely nonplused.

"You say the word, boss," Lefty said, "and . . ."

"Yes, yes," Brandon interrupted eagerly. "Go ahead and say it. Just say it, Carr. Go ahead, say it!"

Carr hesitated a moment, and said suavely. "Do come in and be seated, gentlemen. Let's talk this over."

"There's nothing to talk over," Brandon said. "I'm going to start searching. I'm tired of talk—your talk particularly."

"Now, wait a minute," Carr said. "Let's be reasonable about this." He motioned Lefty to one side, led the way to the living room.

"To hell with being reasonable. *I'm* going to start a search," Brandon said. "I have a force of deputies waiting at my office. I'm going to get on the telephone, call them up here and I'm going to search this house from garret to basement."

Carr said angrily to Selby, "You usually are a lot more astute than this, Counselor. You've placed yourself in a legally vulnerable position."

"You're probably right," Selby said. "I'm taking a gamble. You should be smart enough to realize that I now can't afford to be talked out of that gamble. I've already put my chips down. I can't pick them back up. Therefore, I have to see if I hold the winning hand. In other words, Carr, I'm going to *search* this house."

Carr abruptly turned his back on them, walked over to the big fireplace in the living room, and stood, drumming his fingers nervously on the wooden mantel.

Selby waited a matter of some ten seconds, then said to Brandon, "All right, Rex, telephone your deputies. And, in the meantime, since we don't want to have any misunderstanding about this, you gentlemen will remain right here where we can watch you."

Brandon started toward the telephone.

Abruptly Carr turned and faced them. "Very well, gentlemen," he said in simple dignity, "you win. Would you mind stepping this way?"

"You, too," Brandon said, nodding to the valet. "I'm keeping you in sight."

Lefty said, "I go where A. B. Carr tells me to and only when he tells me to."

"Right at the moment," Brandon said, "you're going where *I* tell you to. You've already gone through the motions of resisting an officer and if you want handcuffs on I'm the man who can put them on."

"It won't be necessary, gentlemen," Carr said wearily. "Come this way. You too, Lefty."

They followed Carr into the corridor, up a flight of stairs, into an upstairs study. Carr unlocked a drawer in the desk, took out a small jewel casket and handed it to the sheriff. "Here are the jewels that you want, I believe, Sheriff."

Brandon looked at the jewels and a sudden surge of triumph came over his face. "Now, my friend," he said, "I'm arresting you for having stolen property in your possession."

"The property," Carr said wearily, "was not stolen. It was turned over to me by way of a fee. I'm afraid that Miss Lennox was hysterical and upset when she reported the burglary to the police. Actually it was not a burglary. The jewels were voluntarily placed in my custody by her some time before the supposed burglary. And I may say, gentlemen, that I consider this whole farcical affair a damnable outrage.

"You know as well as I do that I can't afford to have this house searched. There are things in here that . . . well, I guess, under the circumstances, I'll refrain from making any further comment. You have your jewels, and if you will tell Miss Lennox where you found them, she will advise you that she gave them to me of her own free will. They were not stolen."

"Now that," Brandon said, grinning, "is something you can tell to the judge, Mr. Carr. This property was reported stolen and . . ."

"*Reported* stolen," Carr said sharply. "You can't act merely on a report. If you take me into custody, Sheriff, you're going to have to stake your reputation on the fact that the property was stolen. Actually it wasn't, and if you will let me step to that phone I can convince you that it wasn't in about five minutes."

"How long has this property been in your possession?" Selby asked.

"A matter of some six weeks," Carr said coldly, "and I think under the circumstances I shall refuse to answer any more questions about it. After all, there's a matter of professional confidence involved. Miss Lennox gave me this property as security for a fee."

"You were in my office this evening," Brandon said, "for the purpose of identifying stolen property. You didn't say anything about it at that time."

"I don't have to discuss my private affairs, and I am duty-bound to protect the interests of a client."

"And," Brandon went on, "you had the publisher of a paper with you."

"A friend of mine."

"A friend of long standing?" Selby asked.

"I've known Mr. Paden for some time."

Selby said, "That's the trouble with you, Carr. You came to this community quietly, almost humbly. Ostensibly you were looking only for an opportunity to relax and retire. We let you in. You were grateful. Now you're beginning to take over. You have too many people who are beholden to you. Too many people in key places. And now your friends are moving in."

"Am I responsible for my friends?" Carr asked. "Can't a friend of mine come to this city if he wants to?"

"The trouble is, Carr, you have too many friends."

"The trouble," Carr said bitterly, "is that I have too many enemies."

"Damned if you haven't," Brandon agreed gleefully. "And now, having caught you with stolen property in your possession, it's going to take more than your word to convince me it wasn't stolen. You're under arrest, Carr. You're coming with me. If you come quietly, and Moana Lennox wants to make a retraction of the theft charge, that's all right with me. If you resist this arrest, I'll throw the book at you."

"I'll have bail and be out of your damned jail within twenty minutes of the time you put me in," Carr said angrily.

"I don't think you can do it under half an hour," Brandon told him. "It's going to take a little while to book you and fingerprint you, you know. And since you're on such friendly terms with the press, perhaps you'd like to call in your publisher friend to write up the story. He might like to make some reference to the fact that at last we've found the *genuine* stolen jewelry. Come on, Carr."

Carr hesitated.

Brandon pulled handcuffs from his belt. "Are you coming the easy way, or the hard way?"

Carr looked at Brandon's grim face and suddenly smiled. "Why certainly, Sheriff. I'll come the easy way, of course. Naturally you have the power to do this, if you want to take the chances."

"I'm taking the chances," Brandon told him. "You're going to jail. You may get yourself out in half an hour, but you're sure as hell going to jail."

23

IN BRANDON'S OFFICE THE NEXT MORNING THE TWO COM-
pared notes.

Sheriff Brandon, grinning gleefully, said, "You certainly said a mouthful when you said you never won
anything by being on the defensive, and that you can't
make an omelette without breaking eggs. Lord knows,
though, I hate to think what would have happened if
Carr *hadn't* had those jewels."

"We sure took a chance," Selby admitted, "but from
a political standpoint we were dead pigeons if we hadn't
done something of the sort. . . . You can begin to get
a picture now, Rex."

"Well," Brandon conceded, "we're getting *parts* of
the puzzle which begin to fit together, but it's not any
picture yet."

"It's darn close to a picture," Selby said. "Carr was
using Moana, and at the same time making her pay for
it. He was getting her out of some scrape, but that
shrewd devil was smart enough, and cunning enough,
to plan to kill two birds with one stone."

Brandon said, "Keep talking, Doug."

Selby thought for a few moments, then said, "I think
Moana got herself into some sort of a scrape. I think
that she went to Carr. I think that Carr saw a heaven-
sent opportunity to clean up something else that was

bothering him. In the person of Moana Lennox he had a young woman of good family whose word would be taken as gospel in any case . . ."

There was a knock at the door of Brandon's private office.

"What is it?" Brandon asked.

A deputy said, "Horace Lennox is out here and his sister Moana is with him. He says that it's very important they see you at the earliest possible moment."

"I'll say it's important," Selby grinned. "Rex, it looks as though this is the break we've been waiting for."

Brandon nodded. "Tell them to come in and then see that we're not disturbed for a while. No matter what happens don't let anyone else in."

The deputy nodded, withdrew, and a moment later ushered Horace and Moana Lennox into the office.

Horace said, as soon as the door was closed, "I'm not going to waste any time with preliminaries, gentlemen. My sister told me a story and as soon as I heard it, I knew that it was something she should tell you. I've had some difficulty in getting her to come up here, and I may say that no one—no other member of the family— knows that we're here, or knows Moana's story."

"We were just speculating about what Moana's story must be," Brandon said. "Suppose you sit down and tell us, Moana."

Horace and his sister sat down. "Go ahead, Moana," Horace said.

She looked him over with the hard, green eyes of a trapped animal. There was no sign of tears or of lids swollen from crying. She was still a gambler, still looking for the breaks, and the only reason she was surrendering was because she could find no other alternative.

A hard little schemer, brought to bay, she sized them up with the cold eyes of a professional fighter searching for an opening.

"Go ahead, Moana," Horace urged.

She said, "The only reason that I'm telling you this is because—because I have to."

"I can well understand that," Brandon said, studying her face.

She said, "I went to A. B. Carr. I wanted him to protect me. He's messed everything all up. Now he expects *me* to clear *him*."

"What did you consult him about? Why did you go to see him?" Horace asked. "Go ahead, tell these men the story just as you told it to me."

She said, "I don't know whether you gentlemen know anything about my family background. My mother has made a fetish of respectability. Well, I guess I didn't do so good. Things happened that I just didn't want Mother to know anything about. It all started back in July when Darwin Jerome and I were going to get married. I knew Mother wouldn't approve and I just didn't care. I decided to run away with Darwin and get married.

"He fixed things all up. We told Mother that we were going up to spend the week end with Connie Kerry, and Connie, knowing what we were planning to do, agreed to front for us so that it would appear we were up there, until I could send Mother a telegram announcing that I was Mrs. Darwin Jerome. . . ." She hesitated for a moment, and the look of calculating defiance left her eyes as she contemplated the misty memories of that July night.

"Go on," Horace said impatiently.

She said, "I've always been very fond of Darwin, but he's a heel. I knew he had weak points but he was likable and sophisticated in his whole attitude toward life. He wanted me to take a chance that I wouldn't take, a chance I couldn't take."

"What?" Selby asked.

"On the road to Yuma it turned out that he was already married. He'd married a girl in France when he was overseas. He told me that he knew it would be all right, and that he could send her money and she'd get a French divorce. He was perfectly willing to go ahead and marry me there in Yuma, but I had visions of what would happen. That French girl would learn he had married again. She'd make trouble and—well, you can see what a position I'd be in. The bride of a bigamist—no binding ceremony—and somehow I had an idea that that might be a very bad position to be in with Darwin Jerome. A girl who is going to toss everything away in order to marry Darwin wants to be darn certain she's got him, and that he's tied up good and tight legally."

"So what did you do?" Brandon asked.

She said, somewhat regretfully, "Oh, well, I let my head dominate my heart. I told him nothing doing. I told him to take me back home, and—well, he wanted me to spend the night in Yuma and we had an argument, and that was that. We separated."

"Then what?" Horace prompted.

"Then," she said, "I was in a fix. I simply had to get back, and I had to get where I could communicate with Connie and tell her what had happened. I could have taken the bus, but I knew Darwin would be down at the bus station looking for me. I just left him flat. I started to hitchhike.

"I walked across the bridge over the river into California and saw a lot of cars lined up at the California checking station. I just stood around as though waiting for the car in which I was riding to be cleared. Finally I saw a man with whom I thought I could take a chance. A nice-looking young fellow who was all alone. I walked up to him and—well, anyway, he gave me a ride. He was Frank Grannis.

"Frank Grannis was a perfect gentleman. Naturally I wasn't foolish enough to tell him any of my story or to give him a name. I told him that I had to get to Los Angeles to see about a job, and that I had to be there by nine o'clock in the morning in order to land the job. It was quite a line I handed him. He had planned to stop in Brawley all night, but after he heard my story he decided that he'd keep on driving."

Selby, listening with frowning concentration, said, "Wait a minute. How did Darwin Jerome know that you were riding with Frank Grannis? And as I size things up, he must have known."

She said, "I'm coming to that. Darwin waited around the bus depot at Yuma. When I didn't show up, he finally realized what must have happened. He passed us on the road, driving like the wind. I recognized the car. He must have been going at least eighty-five or ninety miles an hour."

"Well?" Selby asked.

She said, "He wasn't so dumb. He knew that I was going to have to get home to Madison City some way. He thought he stood a chance. There's no question but what Darwin is—or was—completely infatuated with me. He had been looking forward to a marriage ceremony which wouldn't be binding, and a honeymoon which would. I upset his calculations. Darwin is a happy-go-lucky individual, but when it comes to a showdown, and if anyone crosses him, he becomes hard as nails."

"What happened?" Selby asked.

"As it turned out, he thought the reason I'd refused to go ahead was because of some other man who had come between us. When I didn't go to the bus depot, he felt certain—and he's insanely jealous.

"There's a boulevard stop just before you come to Madison City with a bright overhead light. Darwin was waiting there. He spotted us when we drove up. I knew that he had, but Frank Grannis didn't. Frank said he simply couldn't go on and wanted to know where I wanted to get out. I'd been making him sleepy for the last half-hour by repeatedly yawning. I told him to put me out any place and I'd keep on hitchhiking. So he stopped the car at the auto camp. I kissed him good-by— just a friendly kiss, the way a regular hitchhiker would treat a nice boy who had given her a long ride, and started walking ostensibly to invite another ride.

"Darwin, of course, had seen me kiss Frank good-by. He'd seen Frank go to the motel. He was jealous and angry and hurt. He really thought Frank had followed us to Yuma and was the reason I'd refused to marry him. I simply couldn't convince him Frank wasn't an old friend. I slapped his face, and we quarreled again and then finally he took me home.

"He was willing to do that much to keep up appearances. I told Mother that I'd been taken violently ill, and thought I'd better come back home, and the next day I called Connie and fixed things up so that she'd back up my story."

"And how did Carr enter the picture?" Selby asked.

"Well," she said, "you can imagine how I felt when I saw that Grannis had been arrested on a hit-and-run charge. I simply can't imagine how they ever picked on him. I *knew* that he wasn't guilty. Of course, he was talking vaguely about a girl hitchhiker whom he'd picked up and who could give him an alibi. I'd given him a purely fictitious background and made it as vague as possible and—well, you know how it is on a pickup like that. You talk awhile and are more or less impersonal and fuzzy about backgrounds.

"I didn't want to see him convicted wrongfully, and yet I couldn't come out and relate the circumstances without getting myself in an awful mess, and letting Mother know I'd lied to her, and all that, so—well, I went to Carr."

"I see. And what did Carr say?"

She said, "Carr wanted money. I didn't have any money. I told him about my jewelry. Carr suggested that he'd look it over."

"And then what?"

"Carr looked at the jewelry and said that he'd see Grannis got out of it and that I wasn't involved; but he said that he wanted to do it his way and that I was not to come forward with any statement no matter what happened. That suited me all right. And Carr told me that any time within a year when I wanted to redeem the jewelry for a thousand dollars I could have it back, that that would be his fee."

"And what about the burglary?" Selby asked hopefully. "That was Carr's idea so that you wouldn't . . ."

"No," she interrupted, "that was my own idea. I thought that was the best way of accounting for the missing jewelry. I wouldn't have had to say anything about it if it hadn't been that Dorothy Clifton came to visit us. I knew that Mother would want to show her the antique jewelry, the heirlooms which I had. She spoke about the stuff at dinner that night."

"I see," Brandon said, disappointment in his voice. "Carr then really didn't have *anything* to do with that fake burglary?"

"Not a thing."

"Wait until she tells you the rest of it," Horace said. "Go ahead, Moana. Try and be as brief as possible, because these men have work to do."

She said, "Well, Carr reported to me from time to time. Of course, this is a relatively small town and it would never do for people to think that I was consulting Carr. I couldn't go to his house and he doesn't have an office here. Even if he had, I couldn't have gone there. So Carr would telephone me at times and meet me at various places. He finally told me that he'd been trying to get the case against Frank Grannis squared up. That he'd offered to make all sorts of concessions to the authorities down there in Imperial County, but they wouldn't even give him a tumble. I didn't like the way he was talking. I thought perhaps he was trying to give me some sort of a double-cross, and actually accused him of it. But he insisted that he was working for my best interests, and that was all he had in mind, but that it was a difficult job to get the case squared without letting anyone know that he'd located the alibi witness. I could appreciate he was up against a problem there but that's what I was paying him for.

"Finally Carr phoned on Tuesday that he had everything fixed. He said he had a girl who would swear that she had ridden with Grannis. He said she was a Daphne Arcola from Windrift, Montana, and that I was to meet her at the park that night. Carr said he'd try and join us."

"Go ahead," Selby said eagerly. "He arranged to meet you in the park the night that Dorothy came?"

"Yes. I knew that she was going to arrive sometime during the evening, and knew I couldn't get away until after the house had settled down, so I told him that I'd have to find out how things were coming and let him know; that it would be difficult for me to call him. So he said that either he or Daphne Arcola would call me sometime during the evening. Well, she called and I didn't think anyone remembered about it. I told her very briefly I'd meet her and Mr. Carr in the park at eleven-ten. I felt certain everything would be quieted down by that time.

"Well, everything would have been all right only Mother told Dorothy to leave her convertible in the driveway and leave the keys in it; that in case anyone had to take a car out they could move hers. Well, I was afraid that all that noise would waken Dorothy, and of course she was in the guest room, which is right over the driveway. It *would* have to happen that way."

"Go on," Selby said eagerly. "What happened? What happened when you got to the park?"

"Well, I got to the park. Daphne Arcola was waiting on the corner. I recognized her at once from the description, and she got in the car with me. Then we drove to the place in the park where we were to meet Mr. Carr."

"And what happened?"

"We shut off the engine and waited for a minute or two, and then Daphne said she thought she saw someone over in the shadow of some shrubbery. She said she'd go over and take a look. I told her that it was foolish, because if Mr. Carr were there he'd come over to meet us, that he wouldn't expect us to get out and go over into the shadows. But she thought perhaps something had gone wrong and that he was afraid to come out to the automobile, but wanted one of us to come over there.

"She jumped out of the car and ran over into the shadows and I lost her for—oh, I don't know, two or three minutes. I was beginning to get frightened when she suddenly came running back to the car, and said to me, 'Moana, go home just as fast as you can. Don't ever admit to anyone that you've met me, or that you know me, or that you've been out of the house this evening. I'll get in touch with you later on and explain.' And with that she slammed the car door and ran across the grass. Naturally, I was terribly disturbed. I ran over the dirt path in making a hurried turn.

"I wasn't as much frightened as I was angry and upset. I wanted to get the thing over, and I—well, all that mystery, all that intrigue. I seemed to be getting mixed into things deeper and deeper. If it hadn't been for the fact that Mr. Carr always seemed so fatherly, and so dignified, and such a bulwark of strength, and so completely assured of what he was doing—well, I knew all that stuff was wrong and that I was getting into a mess, but—well, Mr. Carr influenced me, that's all."

"Then Daphne Arcola had left her purse in your car, or rather, in Dorothy Clifton's car, and you didn't know it was there?" Selby asked.

She nodded. "I took the machine back and left it in the driveway. I thought I'd worked it so no one would

213

know anything about what had happened. I went into my room, cut a hole in the screen, unhooked the screen, undressed in the dark, got into bed, and then started screaming."

"And that's all you know?" Selby asked.

"That," she said, "is the entire story."

"Did Daphne Arcola get in touch with you later?"

She hesitated a moment, then said, "Yes."

"When?"

"Yesterday. She told me to sit tight, that she and Mr. Carr had everything under control."

"Last night," Selby said, "we had every reason to believe that Carr got Frank Grannis out of jail by temporarily putting up a surety bond. He got him to a place where he could meet Daphne Arcola and there they fixed up a story. Do you know anything about that?"

The hard green eyes regarded Selby with cold appraisal. "Isn't that enough—what I've already told you?"

"I want it all," Selby said. "You've held out too much too long. You should have told us all this sooner."

She said, "You detest me, don't you? And yet I got into all this trouble simply because I tried to be a good sport and help a man out of a predicament. After all, it was nothing in *my* young life. I could have sat tight and said nothing. Then I wouldn't have lost my jewelry and wouldn't have been in all this mess. I wish now I'd *really* been selfish."

"Did you," Selby asked, "see Frank Grannis last night?"

"Yes," she flared defiantly.

"Where?"

"At a motel."

"Who was there?"

"Daphne, A. B. Carr, and some stooge of Carr's. I believe he's a real estate man from Fallhaven."

"And what was the purpose of that conference?"

"To fix it up so Daphne Arcola could tell a convincing story. I told her absolutely everything that had happened, and Frank Grannis told her everything that had happened as he remembered it, and—well, Daphne and Frank sort of got their stories ironed out."

"And Carr was there?" Selby said, unable to keep the triumph from his voice. "He helped in getting this story straightened out, helped in planning this perjury?"

"No," she said. "Carr was at the motel, but he wouldn't have anything to do with the conference. He got us all together and said, 'You folks probably want to visit for a while. When you're finished I'll talk about the case and find out what it's all about so I can prepare my defense,' and then he went out."

Brandon glanced questioningly at Selby.

Selby said, "I believe we can get him for subornation of perjury and criminal conspiracy. But we'll probably need to prove an overt act. We'll have to get Grannis to testify for us. We should be able to do that all right, because now we're in a position to deduce what must have happened, and how that hit-and-run charge was framed on Grannis in the first place. However," Selby went on, "we'd better let that wait until we've made certain Miss Lennox has given us all the facts as she is familiar with them."

Selby turned to Moana. "Do you think there's any possibility that Daphne Arcola killed Rose Furman when she got out of the car?" he asked.

The green eyes met his for a moment, then wavered,

then returned to meet his defiantly. "I don't know. I have no idea what happened."

"She was gone long enough to have committed the murder?"

Moana said scornfully, "How long does it take a person to stick a knife in another person, Mr. Selby?"

Selby acknowledged the point with a smile. "That's not a definite answer to my question, however."

She said, "I'd prefer not to answer the question just as you asked it. She was gone at least three minutes. It seemed longer."

Selby glanced inquiringly at Horace Lennox.

Horace said, "That's all of her story, gentlemen."

"Carr didn't know that you were coming here?" Selby asked.

She shook her head. "No one knows. Horace sweated it out of me. He knew that Dorothy wasn't the one who had driven the car that night and so he—well, he went to work on me."

She glanced at her brother and suddenly there was bitter anger in her eyes. She said jealously, "He's so completely wrapped up in that Dorothy person that he doesn't care what happens to his own sister!"

"It isn't that, Moana," Horace interposed quickly. "I love you, and I love Dorothy. I *knew* Dorothy was innocent. Good Lord, you wouldn't let her become involved in a murder simply to save you from the consequences of gossip, would you?"

She said, "A really *smart* lawyer would fix it so I didn't have to sacrifice myself."

"Perhaps your friend Mr. Carr would," Horace said sarcastically.

She looked at him appraisingly as though seeing him only as an attorney and not as a relative.

"I think perhaps he would," she said. "In fact, I *know* he would. But you dragged the story out of me and then took me up here, and now—now, I'm licked."

Brandon glanced at Selby.

Selby said, "Don't tell your story to anyone for a while, Moana. Just go home and keep your own counsel. The sheriff and I will talk things over and see what can be done. And thanks a lot, Horace, for your co-operation."

"Yes," Moana said, as she arose from the chair she had been occupying, and started for the door. "Thank you very much, Horace, for your co-operation and desire to save your pretty little fiancée—*at no matter what cost to your sister!*"

24

BRANDON PICKED UP THE TELEPHONE, SAID TO THE OPER-
ator, "Rush through a call to the sheriff's office at El
Centro. I'll hold the line. Put it through as a police
emergency."

A moment later Brandon said, "Hello. This is Brandon at Madison City. About this prisoner, Frank
Grannis, I have reason to believe he's innocent of that
hit-and-run charge. I think he was framed on that, but
he can be of a lot of help to us on a case we're working
on up here; a murder case, and there's a question of
subornation of perjury in connection with it. Now you
might get in touch with him and explain to him that
if he wants to co-operate we'll try to dig up proof that
will get him out of the charge down there. We'll show
you that you really have the wrong party and . . .
what's that? When?

"I see. All right. Well then, I guess that's that.
Good-by."

Brandon hung up the telephone, turned to Selby and
said, "Too late again."

"What happened?"

"Carr rang up the judge at seven-thirty this morning,
told him there'd been some trouble with the surety bond
and talked the judge into making a new order for one
thousand dollars' cash bail. Carr had a local attorney on

the ground with the cash within ten minutes of the time the new bail order was made. Frank Grannis walked out of jail over an hour ago. With the stakes Carr's playing for, a thousand dollars is a drop in the bucket. He'll toss that away and think nothing of it. We'll never find Grannis. Not now."

Brandon slumped down in the chair. "Damn the guy. He always seems to be one jump ahead of us."

Selby, snuggling the warm bowl of his pipe in his hand, started walking the floor, from time to time putting the pipe to his mouth for a few thoughtful puffs.

"Now," he said, "the thing begins to make a pattern we can follow and understand. Darwin Jerome, intensely jealous, driving like a madman, trying to beat Moana Lennox back to Madison City, hits a cyclist on a lonely, deserted section of the road across the sand dunes from Yuma to El Centro.

"We can probably give him credit for having stopped to investigate. He found he'd killed a Mexican cyclist and that there was nothing he could do by way of giving aid. So he got back in his car and speeded on toward Madison City.

"He got there and waited for Moana. He found her driving with a man who actually was a stranger; but Darwin was hurt and jealous and thought that man had followed them and was the real reason Moana had jilted him. He knew that this man had been over the same road he had traveled, and he knew that Moana would never dare to come forward and give him an alibi. In order to do that she'd have to ruin her reputation. So Darwin did a clever thing as far as he's concerned. He knew the motel where Grannis was staying. He waited until he was certain Grannis was asleep, then he took an iron bar, dented a fender and broke off a piece from the right headlight lens, being as silent as possible. Then he drove back to the place where the accident had occurred. It was probably daylight by that time, so he had no trouble finding the place. He dropped the piece from Grannis's headlight by the body, where it was certain to be found, and then telephoned the sheriff's office at El Centro that there was a dead man over in the dunes, and gave the approximate mileage.

"By that simple expedient Jerome put Moana in a spot, got out of his own difficulty, and put a potential rival in jail.

"Moana's conscience bothered her. She went to A. B. Carr. Carr is a clearinghouse for criminal cases. He saw a chance to clear up some case that had been bothering him, by tying it onto Moana's case. Now then, Rex, I think the murder is connected with that other case and I think we're only going to solve the murder when we find out what that case was."

"How can we find out?"

"It's a case Rose Furman was working on. She was a detective. We've found out she was working on two cases but both of those apparently were closed. She could have had other cases. Something that was pretty close to home as far as old A. B. Carr was concerned."

Brandon said, "I'm with you all the way, Doug, except that I go a lot further. I think she was working on a case involving Carr, and I think Carr knew about it, and I think he made an appointment to meet Moana and Daphne Arcola, and then when he found out Rose Furman was following him, he slipped a knife into her back and . . ."

"Wait a minute," Selby said. "How do we know, Rex, that both of those cases Rose Furman was working on *were* cleaned up?"

"Well, both clients told us so."

"And how did they know?"

"They'd received reports from Rose Furman."

"But had they?"

"What do you mean? She'd left a note in the type-writer in one case and sent a telegram in the other."

"How do we know she did? We don't have her signature on either one. There's a telegram for one thing, and a typewritten note for another. Where are her signatures?"

Brandon came bolt upright in his chair. "Where was that telegram sent from, Doug?"

"Corona. Of course, the assumption is that she sent the telegram, then went to her apartment, wrote the letter, and then started back for Madison City. But that letter *could* have been written in her apartment and the telegram sent later on from Corona as she was on her way back to Madison City. Now the question is, what brought her back?"

"A. B. Carr," Brandon said positively.

"Let's investigate and see what we can find out," Selby said. "First rattle out of the box, let's find out from Corona about the person who sent that wire. It may have been a man."

"What's holding us back?" Brandon said enthusiastically. "Now we're on the right track."

"You have some pictures of Rose Furman?"

"That's right. Come on, let's get started."

They went pell-mell down the Courthouse steps.

Harry Elrod, *The Blade* reporter, came running toward them. "What is it, boys?" he asked. "Have you got a tip?"

They ignored him, but pushed on through the back door of the Courthouse into the official parking space.

Elrod, running along behind, shouted, "Hey, what's it all about? What's . . ."

They jumped into the sheriff's car. The doors slammed.

Elrod made a dash for his own car, climbed in, and started the motor.

The sheriff, watching out of the corner of his eye, said, "This is going to be good. We'll let him try to follow us."

He gunned the powerful motor into life, switched on the red spotlight, and threw on the siren. "I don't ordinarily go in for all this fanfare of trumpets, Doug," he said, with a quiet grin, "but if that reporter wants to follow me in the jalopy *The Blade* provides as transportation for its reporters, he's going to have *quite* a ride."

The car rocketed through town, passed frozen traffic at the street intersections, out onto the main highway toward Los Angeles, and then settled down to steady, throbbing speed.

From time to time Brandon glanced in the rearview mirror, then finally relaxed with a smile. "He probably thought we were going some place in town. When we took him out on the main highway he was hopelessly lost. Probably bogged down in the traffic."

Brandon adjusted himself more comfortably in the driver's seat, gave attention to driving the car until he screamed into Corona.

The telegraph operator in the railroad station in

Corona remembered the occasion of the wire perfectly.

"It was a girl," he said. "A young woman. A cute, red-haired girl with a nice figure."

Brandon's face fell. "You're sure she's the one?"

"That's right."

"How was the wire written?" Selby asked. "In handwriting, or . . ."

"No, it had been written on a typewriter. I remember that. I can dig into the files and find it, I guess. It was all written on a typewriter. I'm certain of that."

"This the woman?" Brandon asked, showing him Rose Furman's picture.

"I think it was. Of course, it's hard to tell. There's something sort of . . . yes, I think it was. Of course, her red hair doesn't show in the picture, and . . . yes, I guess it's the woman all right."

"Well," Brandon said to Selby, "I guess that knocks that theory into a cocked hat."

They thanked the telegraph operator, started back to the county car.

"Hang it," Brandon grumbled. "I thought we were on the right track. We must have . . ."

"Wait a minute," Selby said, as he noticed a copy of the evening *Blade* in the rear of the car.

A photograph of Daphne Arcola smiled up at Selby from the front page under headlines reading, DISTRICT ATTORNEY SELBY INVADED BEDROOM WITNESS CLAIMS.

"Just a minute, Rex," Selby said. "Let's try this thing from another angle. You remember it was the resemblance between these two women that touched off the initial mistake in this case when we thought Daphne Arcola was the one who had been killed."

Selby picked up the newspaper, walked back to the

telegraph office, and said, "Now *this* girl has red hair. Of course this is a newspaper photograph and . . ."

"*That's* the one," the operator exclaimed unhesitatingly. "I *know* that's the one. I recognize her. That's it. She is the one who sent the telegram. There's a resemblance between her and the other girl, but this is the one."

Selby grinned across at Brandon. "Now let's find out where Daphne Arcola is. We're getting somewhere."

"Want me to call the office?" Brandon asked.

"Let's call Sylvia Martin at *The Clarion*," Selby said. "She can go around as a news reporter and it won't attract so much attention. She'll say she wants an interview."

"Sure," Brandon said. "Go to it."

Selby put through a call from the phone in the station, in order to expedite matters, making it a station-to-station call to the office of the Madison *Clarion*.

"Hello," he said, when he had an operator on the line. "This is Doug Selby, the district attorney. I want to talk with Sylvia Martin. It's important, and . . ."

The operator interrupted to say, "She's been trying to get you too, Mr. Selby. She's on some sort of a hot tip. One of the persons in whom you're interested, and who Sylvia thinks has a key to the situation, was leaving in an automobile on some mysterious errand. Sylvia was trying to get you so that you could follow. When she couldn't find you, she started out in her own car."

Selby said, "Well, I guess we can't wait then."

He hung up and explained the situation to Brandon. "Daphne must be skipping out, Rex. Sylvia's trying to trail her."

Brandon said, "What'll we do, Doug?"

"Broadcast a pickup on Daphne Arcola, Rex."

Brandon called his office and said to the deputy who answered the phone, "Find out where Daphne Arcola is, and nail her down. If she's left town, send out a pickup. If she hasn't left, but starts to go anywhere, put her in custody. If Carr tries to get bail for her, see that things are tied up until we can get there. We're starting from Corona right now."

Brandon hung up the telephone, said, "Let's go."

They climbed in the car and in a matter of minutes were speeding over the road at seventy miles an hour.

Suddenly Selby grabbed Brandon's knee. "Hold it, Rex. That's A. B. C.'s car coming down that hill on the road ahead."

Brandon said, "Darned if it isn't. I'd know that battleship on wheels anywhere."

Brandon slowed the car, extended his arm from the window, made signals.

Old A. B. C. ignored the signals. His big sedan, hurtling along the highway, went whipping past with such speed that the suction of air rocked the county car.

Brandon said, "The dirty shyster," and watching his opportunity spun his car in a complete turn.

"That was Daphne Arcola with him," Selby said.

"We'll get them," Brandon promised.

The county car rolled into speed. Ahead, the road became a divided highway. There was no sign of the car they were pursuing.

Brandon floorboarded the throttle. They roared along the smooth cement ribbon.

"There he is," Selby said. "I recognize the rear of his car. The bumper's chromium plated, but it's railroad iron. They say the windows are bulletproof."

Brandon slowly cut the distance.

A. B. Carr was giving his big machine plenty of gas and was passing cars with such regularity that he consistently hugged the left-hand lane. Brandon nursed his car up behind the lawyer's car. Then, watching for an opportunity, suddenly shot over into the right-hand lane and floorboarded the throttle.

After a second, the two cars were abreast. Old A. B. Carr at the wheel glanced across, saw the sheriff's automobile, recognized Selby, and abruptly pushed his own throttle down to the floorboard.

The powerful motor sent the car surging forward, but Brandon, jamming the throttle of the county car wide open, kept alongside. However, the advantage was Carr's because Carr was in the left lane of traffic, and as a big truck and trailer loomed ahead of the county car in the right-hand lane, Brandon was trapped.

For a moment the sheriff hesitated, then, giving the machine everything he had, started cutting to the left.

The truck and trailer were being overtaken with such rapidity that they drew measurably closer with each swift second while Carr's machine, which had slowly started to forge ahead, still couldn't make it far enough to draw away from the county car.

Selby braced himself.

Brandon grimly swung the wheel over more and more to the left until there was a scant half-inch between the fenders of the two cars.

Old A. B. Carr lost his nerve at the showdown. He took his foot off the throttle. Brandon's car, cutting in between the wide truck and trailer and the speeding car of the lawyer, seemed to have less than an inch to spare on each side. But the sheriff was now ahead of the other machine. He grinned, shifted one hand, pulled out his revolver from its holster, placed it on the seat beside him, and slowed down, waiting for Carr to come up.

Old A. B. C. refused to take the invitation. He slowed his machine abruptly.

Brandon slammed on the brakes, watching developments in the rearview mirror.

Carr veered over to the right, but Brandon refused to walk into that trap. He eased his machine only part way over so that when Carr suddenly tried to detour back to the left, Brandon had forestalled him and the county machine was ahead, all the time slowing in speed, forcing Carr over to the right-hand lane.

The truck and trailer coming behind started a raucous blast of its horn; then the driver, sizing up the situation, as he noted the tax-exempt license on the county car, swung over to the right and started slowing down.

Carr made a last desperate effort to scrape by on the right and Brandon, driving with his left hand, holding the gun in his right, swerved the car over sharply forcing A. B. C. off the road.

Carr brought his machine to a stop, raised his hat in a courtly bow, and said, "Good morning, gentlemen, good morning. Aren't you rather hogging the traffic, Sheriff? It seemed to me you wanted pretty much all of the road."

"No," Brandon said dryly, "just the part that you were on. Pull over there and shut off your motor."

"I say," Carr protested, "I'm in rather a hurry and . . ."

"You're being stopped for questioning," Brandon

said, "and if you try to get away I'm going to start shooting the tires out."

"Well, of course," Carr said, smiling affably, "if you want to be arbitrary and violent about it. Aren't you outside of your county, however, Sheriff?"

"I'm outside of my county and within my rights."

"After all," Carr announced, "so far as the law is concerned, there are several . . ."

Brandon raised the gun. "Carr," he said, "you try to make a getaway and I'll riddle your tires. Now if you can get a writ of habeas corpus that'll keep a bullet from penetrating rubber, you'd better get one fast, because you're going to need it."

Carr surrendered with a good-natured laugh, said, "Well, well, since you're so remarkably insistent, Sheriff, I suppose there's no alternative but to consume more of my valuable time in listening to your questions—questions which so frequently are completely beside the point. But go right ahead, Sheriff, if it'll give you any pleasure, let's get it out of your system."

"I want to talk with Daphne Arcola," Brandon said, getting out of the car and holstering his revolver.

Carr's lips tightened. "What questions did you want to ask Miss Arcola?"

"Where are you going, for one thing," Brandon said.

"I received a call which is taking me to my office in the city."

"You put up bail for Frank Grannis earlier today, I believe," Selby said.

"That's right, I did. Is there any law against that?"

"*Why* did you put up that bail?"

"Because he's a client of mine," Carr said, "and I'm satisfied he's innocent. I feel that he's been given a raw

228

deal. I put up my own money as bail and I don't have to answer . . ."

"And then where did he go when he left El Centro?"

"Good heavens, gentlemen, *I* don't know," Carr said. "I asked him to keep in touch with me, naturally. And, of course, when the time is set for his trial he'll be there. Otherwise, of course, I'd have to forfeit the bail money." And Carr smiled blandly.

"All right," Brandon said, turning to Daphne Arcola. "Why did *you* go into the telegraph office at Corona and send a wire to Mrs. Barker C. Nutwell in Los Angeles and sign the name of Rose Furman, the murdered girl?"

Daphne Arcola's eyes widened. Her face suddenly drained of color so that the patches of rouge showed distinctly orange.

Carr flashed her a swift glance, and said, "Don't answer that question, Daphne."

"If you don't answer it, I'll take you into custody," Brandon warned.

"On what charge, may I ask?"

"You may," Brandon said grimly.

"May what?"

"May ask."

Carr said, "In the first place, you're out of your county, Sheriff. In the second place, if you try to make an arrest, I shall insist upon having the prisoner informed of the charge against her, and then I shall insist upon the prisoner being immediately taken before the nearest and most accessible magistrate in order that bail may be fixed."

"Which, I suppose, you'll put up," Brandon said.

"I might," Carr said. "I'm financially able to do so."

He reached in his pocket, pulled out a wallet, and started taking out thousand-dollar bills.

There was that in the gesture which indicated that if Brandon so elected he might have received some of the contents of the wallet.

Brandon's face darkened. He pushed Carr to one side, reached in past the steering wheel, took Daphne Arcola by the wrist, and said, "Get out. You're under arrest."

"For what?" she asked.

"I'll tell you what the charge is when I get good and ready," Brandon said.

"For forging the name of Rose Furman to a telegram," Selby said hastily.

"Thank you, Counselor," A. B. Carr said. "She's arrested on a charge of forgery. That's an offense for which bail can be fixed. Now if you will take the prisoner before the nearest and most accessible magistrate, I'll put up her bail, and . . ."

"All right," Brandon said, "we'll take her in on a charge of murder then."

"Murder!" Carr exclaimed.

"That's right. You force my hand and see what you get," Brandon said.

"You're not going to take this young woman into custody in this county," Carr said.

Brandon produced his handcuffs. "I'm going to take this woman into custody," he said, "and if you resist an officer in the discharge of his duties, I'm going to take you into custody."

"You can't do it," Carr said, pushing his way forward. "You're outside your jurisdiction. You have no authority in this county, you're acting without a warrant, you're making an illegal arrest, and you're refusing to take the prisoner before the nearest and most accessible magistrate. All are distinct violations of the law."

"So what!" Brandon said. "Do you want me to hand-cuff this girl to my wrist and then let you try to get her loose with a lot of legal flimflam?"

"I appeal to the district attorney of Madison County," A. B. Carr said.

Brandon said, *"I'm* arresting this young woman. Get into the car, Miss Arcola."

Carr stepped forward. "Don't do it."

Brandon whirled to face Carr. "Just try putting a hand on her or on me. Just so much as a finger."

Brandon piloted Daphne over to the county car and said, "Do you want to get in under your own power, or do you want to be lifted in? Do you want to ride like a lady, or do you want to be handcuffed?"

Carr raised his voice. "Miss Arcola, this arrest is illegal. I advise you not to answer any questions, and I advise you not to submit to any questioning. I advise you to keep absolutely silent and there's one more thing I . . ."

Carr crowded forward as though about to whisper some confidential instructions to the young woman.

Brandon suddenly whirled. His shoulder caught Carr in the chest sending him spinning back.

"Watch that girl, Doug," Brandon said, and strode after the reeling lawyer. "Now then," he said, "you and I are about of an age. Do you want to make an issue of this, or don't you?"

Carr suddenly recovered his dignity and his affa-bility. "Certainly not in terms of personal violence, my dear Sheriff. Whatever *I* do will be done legally," he said. And with that he got in his machine, started the motor, and once more started speeding along the road to Los Angeles.

Brandon walked around and climbed in behind the wheel of the county car. Selby got in beside Daphne Arcola in the front seat. Brandon started to turn the car.

Selby said, "Why did you send that telegram, Miss Arcola?"

She clamped her lips in a firm, thin line of determination.

Selby said, "Let's not take her back to Madison City right now, Rex. Let's take her to Corona and let this man identify her."

"Isn't that illegal?" Daphne Arcola asked.

Brandon grinned, and said, "It always takes a crook to talk about the legalities of a situation."

They drove back to Corona. Daphne Arcola sat frozen-faced in the automobile while the clerk of the Western Union came out, looked at her, and said, "That's the one. She's trying to look different by holding her face all frosty and cold. When she was in here she was all smiles, but that's the girl all right."

"She's the one that sent the telegram?"

"That's right."

Selby grinned at Brandon. "Okay, Rex, *now* let's head back to Madison City. But first let's get that telegram."

"I have it for you," the clerk said. "I looked it up after you left. I was able to find it. Here's the telegram just the way she brought it in."

Selby glanced at the typewriting, frowned, and said, "It was filed a short time *before* Rose Furman was murdered. Whoever wrote it out must have been planning the murder at that time. It will show premeditation. Now, unless I'm mistaken, Rex, this was *not* written on Rose Furman's typewriter, the one that was in her apartment. That's a portable. This seems to have been written on another machine. Now this . . . wait a minute, Rex."

"What is it?" the sheriff asked.

Selby said, "Put yourself in old A. B. Carr's position. What would he normally have done?"

"What do you mean?"

Selby said, "Daphne Arcola is mixed up in this thing. Her testimony can be damaging to old A. B. C. Ordinarily he would have moved heaven and earth to get her out of jail as soon as she was put in."

"Well, he tried his best," Brandon said, grinning. "At least he tried to move me."

"No, he didn't, Rex. He tried to bluff us out of arresting her but after that he didn't do a thing. He quit cold and went tearing on down the highway toward Los Angeles. Ordinarily he'd have followed along, yapping at our heels, demanding that we take her before the nearest and most accessible magistrate, get bail fixed, and . . ."

"Okay," Brandon said, "I get it. What do we do, Doug?"

"We get to Los Angeles just as fast as we can," Selby said.

Daphne Arcola interposed hotly, "I have *some* rights! You can't drag me around all over the country wherever you happen to want . . ."

"Better quit talking and find something to hang hold of, sister," Brandon told her. "As things stand right now, you're about to have the ride of your life."

233

25

SELBY LOOKED AT HIS WATCH, MADE A MENTAL CALCULA-
tion. "We can't make it, Rex. We'll have to telephone."

Brandon slowed the car. "Okay, what do we do?"

Selby said, "The next public phone we see rush
through a call to Bert Hardwick at the Los Angeles
sheriff's office. Tell him to pick up Barton Mosher. Tell
him not to make any charge unless he has to, but, in
case he has to, to charge him with the murder of Rose
Furman. And just to make a good job, charge him with
the murder of Carl Remerton."

Brandon glanced sidelong at Selby to see whether the
district attorney meant what he said, or was merely
putting on an act for the benefit of Daphne Arcola.
Then, spying the sign of a pay phone ahead, he abruptly
braked the car.

While Brandon was phoning, Selby settled himself in
the cushions of the car, filled his pipe.

Daphne Arcola said, *"You* don't have to be so tough.
Perhaps if you'd act a little more human you might find
there was more percentage in it."

Selby turned toward her, started to say something,
then suddenly reached for the siren button as he saw
Sylvia Martin's light press car rocketing along, trying
to make speed.

At the sound of the siren she risked a sidelong glance,

then threw on brakes, brought the car to a weaving stop.

"Well, well, the press," Daphne Arcola said, as Sylvia Martin parked the car and came racing back. "I presume this is entirely accidental."

Sylvia ran up to the county car. "Oh, Doug, I'm so glad to see you I could kiss you. Old A. B. C. headed for Los Angeles.and he took . . ." She suddenly broke off as she saw Daphne Arcola.

"Hop in, Sylvia," Selby invited. "Get in the back seat. Your car should be all right there."

She opened the door on the rear, jumped in.

"I *thought* we lacked something," Daphne said sarcastically. "*Now* we're all fixed, friendly press, everything!"

Brandon returned to the car, grinning. "I got Hardwick himself, Doug. You know what'll happen. He'll really go to town."

"That's fine," Selby said. "It was a break getting Hardwick personally. Now we can relax. Old A. B. C. will walk right into the trap."

"Better tell me a few things," Brandon said, then catching sight of Sylvia Martin, "Why, hello, Sylvia. How did you get here—fly?"

"Darn near," she said.

"Good to see you. Wish you'd arrived sooner. Go on, Doug, just what *did* happen?"

Daphne Arcola missed the sidelong glance the sheriff gave the district attorney.

"We can deduce what happened now, Rex," Selby said. "Carl Remerton went to Windrift, Montana. He was a liberal spender. I wouldn't doubt if perhaps old A. B. Carr has a finger in the pie in Mosher's gambling outfit up there, and I presume you, Daphne, were a professional come-on."

"Save your breath," she said acidly. "Don't waste it asking me questions."

"That's what must have happened," Selby said. "Daphne took Carl Remerton in tow. She saw that he had plenty of action and that he kept going to Barton Mosher's place. Mosher saw that he lost plenty. Then Remerton became suspicious and they had to get rid of him."

Selby stole a swift glance at Daphne Arcola.

"Or," he went on, "something happened and they decided to give him knockout drops and that finished his heart.

"In the meantime, his sister hired a detective to find out what had happened. That really bothered Mosher. The fat was in the fire.

"Now notice a peculiar coincidence. One of those things that isn't entirely a coincidence because with a man who has as much practice as old A. B. Carr there are undoubtedly cases which dovetail, and dates which coincide time after time. But Carl Remerton met his death on July twenty-ninth. Daphne Arcola was mixed up in that death, and so was Barton Mosher. They appealed to Carr when Rose Furman got on the job. Then Moana Lennox came to Carr and wanted a man freed on a hit-and-run charge. He was really innocent and Moana knew it but couldn't testify. The date was the twenty-ninth of July. Obviously, if Carr could give Daphne Arcola an alibi by showing that she was in California on the evening of the twenty-ninth, she could hardly have been administering knockout drops to Carl Remerton on that same date in Windrift, Montana.

"Now, you can piece together all of the things that Carr did. He convinced Moana that, as her benefactor, he'd get someone to take her place as an alibi witness. If he had offered to do this for nothing, it would have made her feel that there was something phony about the deal, and that Carr had an ax to grind. So Carr got her to part with something of value. All that she had was the antique jewelry. It wasn't anything that Carr would ordinarily have bothered with. Carr didn't even plan to dispose of it. He simply intended to keep it so as to make his activities appear regular so far as Moana was concerned."

"Go on, Doug," Brandon said. "You're doing fine."

"Well, there you have the entire story," Selby went on. "You'll remember, Rex, that when we first started figuring the thing we felt that Carr wanted to get an alibi for someone or something. Then it looked as though we were wrong and he was giving someone an alibi. But, Carr was up to his old tricks."

"And you think Carr killed Rose Furman?"

Selby said, "Carr doesn't resort to murder. He isn't that crude, but I wouldn't put it at all past Carr to have suggested to Mosher that as long as Rose Furman was on the job he was bound to end up behind the eight ball sooner or later."

"And where does that leave this girl?" Brandon asked, motioning his head toward Daphne Arcola.

"Probably," Selby said, "she's the one who put the knockout drops in the drink, or whatever it was. We'll have to get an order exhuming the body and have a delicate chemical analysis made. But my best guess is Carl Remerton was murdered, either deliberately, or killed accidentally, in the process of seeing that he was kept quiet when he found out that he'd been trimmed and started to make a complaint.

"I'm not so certain that we can definitely prove our case against Mosher, but we certainly have the goods on this girl—or will have after we go into the question of Remerton's death—and people of Mosher's type are always rats. They'll grab at straws. That's what Carr was so intent upon doing. He was going to save his own skin while he still had a chance. He was going to get in touch with Mosher and—well, it's a two to one bet, Rex, that they were going to fix things up so that Mosher turned state's evidence and got off scot-free, and this girl got the works. That's Mosher's type."

Selby stole a sidelong glance at Daphne Arcola's profile, then went on. "And it's a dirty shame in a way, because girls like Daphne get by on their beauty and youth. You know what happens after a woman has served a term in prison, even if it's only a five-year term. She comes out looking like an old hag. There's nothing left for her except jobs of floor scrubbing and they're lucky to get those. Inside of another five years they have the figure of a sack of potatoes and . . ."

"Stop it!" Daphne Arcola screamed at him.

Selby looked at her in surprise. "What's wrong, Daphne, can't you take it?"

"Of course I can't take it. And neither could any other woman. But I'm beginning to realize a lot of things now. You say Mosher would make a deal to turn state's evidence and get off scot-free?"

Selby nodded.

"Well," she said, "how about beating him to it? If you want a witness, I'll make you a proposition."

Selby said, "I can't *guarantee* anything, but we'd use our influence with the grand jury, *if* the facts warrant it."

She said, "Well, you seem to know pretty much what happened. The only thing you have wrong is my part.

"I was a come-on girl all right and I saw that Carl Remerton got taken to the cleaners. He was a good sport and a free spender, but, believe me, when he thought he'd been gypped, he really was a fighting fool.

"That's where Mosher made his mistake. He underestimated Remerton, but I wasn't the one who gave him the doped drink. I was instructed to get him in touch with Mosher that night. In other words, to put him on the spot. I thought it was just another gambling deal. Then I was instructed to leave him. I knew something was fishy then. The next I knew he was supposed to have died of heart failure while he was driving his automobile. Naturally, I kept my own counsel.

"Then Mosher told me this woman detective was on the job, that the man's sister was making trouble, that it looked as though I might be framed with having given him knockout drops, or something. So then I suggested we come to Madison City and get in touch with A. B. Carr. My friend, Babe Harlan, married Carr, and had told me all about him . . . and got herself a pretty soft berth.

"I wrote Carr. He wired he'd meet me. I called Carr's house and tried to talk with his wife. I didn't let her know that I had any business with old A. B. C. I left a message knowing that that would give A. B. C. his cue.

"Well, Carr called me and told me to call Moana Lennox, to meet her, and be at the park at a certain time. We were to meet him there.

"We got to the park and—well, I found Rose Furman's body. Then suddenly I realized that instead of providing me with an alibi, they had put me right in

239

the middle of a murder rap. By that time there was nothing I could do.

"But I know what I'm going to do now. I'm going to sing my way out of it."

"Did Carr ever say anything that led you to believe he knew about the murder?"

She said, "Mosher stuck the knife in her. We all knew that, but Carr never *said* anything."

Selby said, "Well, Rex, I guess we have our murder case solved, but pinning anything on old A. B. C. depends on whether Mosher decides to sit tight."

"Mosher," she said positively, "will do whatever A. B. C. tells him."

"Old A. B. C. may not have a chance to tell him anything—for a while," Selby said.

Sylvia Martin spoke up timidly from the back seat. "*Could* you put me out at the nearest pay telephone sign you see? I'll get home somehow, and I simply *have* to telephone *The Clarion*. I think the publisher would like to get out an extra that would hit the streets at the same time as *The Blade* goes on sale."

Rex Brandon thought that over, a slow grin spread over his features. "Now *that's* an idea, Sylvia."

Brandon suddenly swerved the car and applied brakes. "Here's a phone, Sylvia."

Selby said, "When you've phoned in your story, go back out to where you left your car and wait for me. I'll ride back with you, if you want a passenger."

She squeezed his hand. The car stopped. Selby held the door open for her.

"Okay, Doug, see you later," she said. "Good-by, and thanks—everyone."

"Fall dead," Daphne Arcola snapped.

26

IT WAS AFTER THREE-THIRTY WHEN REX BRANDON PULLED the county car off to the side of the road and Selby getting out, waved good-by to the sheriff and walked over to Sylvia Martin's car.

"Have any trouble getting back here, Sylvia?" he asked.

"I hitchhiked."

"Been waiting long?"

"Uh-huh. What happened?"

"Well," Selby said, "we have the murder solved."

"Doug, how did you get your original hunch on Mosher? Only I know it wasn't a hunch, but the result of good honest thought."

He laughed. "It was both thought and hunch, Sylvia. Notice that Rose Furman supposedly gave Daphne Arcola a clean bill of health and then gave Remerton a virtual certificate of death from natural causes. Yet she never signed either document.

"She must have found out about Remerton before she arrived in Los Angeles. The phony wire from Corona was sent only a short time before her death.

"Why wouldn't she have telephoned her client instead of wiring? Supposedly she was whisked away from Los Angeles in such a hurry she didn't have time to finish her report to Mosher. Yet it was really all finished.

And why didn't she telephone Mrs. Nutwell as a follow-up on the wire?

"If we once start questioning the truth of statements contained in those unsigned documents, we realize that Rose Furman's murderer could well have secured her purse. He could have then gone to Los Angeles and entered the apartment. All he needed was to have some accomplice send that Corona telegram.

"What murderer? What accomplice? Obviously the two suspects who had been so fortuitously 'cleared' by Rose Furman before her death would have had a motive. When we remember that both of the documents by which Rose Furman cleared them were unsigned, the situation becomes suspicious."

"But, Doug, isn't it strange that Mosher would have murdered her so Daphne would have stumbled on the body, and . . . ?"

"No," Selby interrupted, "that's where the pattern of the crime shows up. Mosher got Daphne to send the wire from Corona and to pose as Rose Furman. Then he brought her back to Madison City.

"Rose promptly picked Daphne up and started following her. That was what Mosher had been planning on. He wanted to lure Rose into the park so he could kill her. The best way was to send Daphne to the park. He knew Rose would follow Daphne and that would put Rose on the spot, right where he wanted her, all ready for the kill."

"And that murder weapon being found in the hedge?"

"That was where Mosher left it. He naturally wanted it to implicate Dorothy. It was, of course, dead easy for the murderer to plant the weapon there."

Sylvia thought that over, nodded. "It all fits all right, Doug. I suppose Mosher grabbed Rose Furman's purse right after he'd stabbed her?"

"That's right. Remember Carr kept asking if we'd found her purse. Carr *must* have known Mosher had taken the purse, and he was questioning us about it to see if we realized the object of the theft—not money but to get car keys, apartment keys, and then leave the purse planted in the dead woman's apartment so as to give an air of authenticity to the typed documents.

"I don't think Carr knew Mosher was going to kill Rose Furman, but Carr went down there to the park to meet Moana and Daphne. It's a pretty good chance he stumbled on the body, probably after Moana had driven back home."

"Then you're going to get Carr?"

"Darned if I know, Sylvia. But we're going to give him a chase. So far our case against him is shrewd conjecture, and that's not evidence. But we're trying to get the evidence dug up so we can use it."

"It seems to me you have him cornered, Doug. If Mosher should confess . . ."

Selby interrupted. "It isn't that simple, Sylvia. As nearly as we can put the facts together, Carr went tearing off toward Los Angeles as soon as we removed Daphne Arcola from his machine. But he was too smart to try racing with us. He did the same thing we did."

"Telephoned?"

Selby nodded. "Evidence shows that Barton Mosher received a mysterious and very urgent telephone call. Immediately after receiving that, he left his hotel and thereupon he seems to have vanished from the face of the earth."

"But you can find him, can't you, Doug? Won't the . . ."

Selby said, "We'll probably get him, but when we do get him we'll have lost our most valuable weapon."

"What?"

"Surprise."

"And how about Daphne Arcola?"

"Daphne Arcola," Selby said, "has changed her mind again and has decided to sit tight. She even denies having made the confession she did make on the road in. She's now claiming we fabricated that. That's going to make you an important witness, Sylvia. I want you to write down exactly what your recollection is of her . . ."

"You dope!" Sylvia interrupted. "What do you think I was doing while she was talking?"

"You mean you took it down?" Selby asked.

"Every word of it," she said.

A smile spread over Selby's face. "Sylvia, you're a wonder, a darling."

Her eyes were troubled. "You mean as a witness?" she said.

"As a woman—not a witness."

There was a breathless catch to her laughter. "I'm glad you found that out, Doug."

"What?"

"That I'm a woman."

"I've known it for *quite* a little while," he told her, "only I've been too busy to talk about it. And now, Sylvia, if you'll just turn the wheel of this automobile directly around, we'll head back to Los Angeles and if we can find music and . . ."

"Oh, Doug, I'd love to, but you know we can't."

"Why not?"

"Well, there's the paper, for one thing, and this case for another."

Selby said, "You've already phoned your story to your paper and, thanks to Rex Brandon, I have been elected to stay in Los Angeles and direct the search for Mosher at least for the next twenty-four hours. And we have every reason to believe we'll catch him before then. And of course you'll want to cover that story. It'll be something we'll have to wait out, so we may as well wait it out where there's dance music and good food. Good old Rex fixed it up with the sheriff's office so that I am to be quote available unquote."

She thought that over for a moment, then turned the wheel of her car. "All right, Doug," she said, "under the circumstances I guess *I'd* better be quote available unquote."

Other Books by ERLE STANLEY GARDNER. . . .
"the most popular whoduniter of his times" *

THE PERRY MASON CASES
THE CASE OF THE

VELVET CLAWS	LAME CANARY
SULKY GIRL	SUBSTITUTE FACE
HOWLING DOG	SHOPLIFTER'S SHOE
LUCKY LEGS	PERJURED PARROT
CURIOUS BRIDE	ROLLING BONES
COUNTERFEIT EYE	BAITED HOOK
CARETAKER'S CAT	HAUNTED HUSBAND
SLEEPWALKER'S NIECE	DROWNING DUCK
SILENT PARTNER	BURIED CLOCK
EMPTY TIN	DROWSY MOSQUITO
CARELESS KITTEN	CROOKED CANDLE
STUTTERING BISHOP	GOLDDIGGER'S PURSE
BLACK-EYED BLONDE	HALF-WAKENED WIFE
DANGEROUS DOWAGER	BORROWED BRUNETTE
FAN-DANCER'S HORSE	LAZY LOVER
LONELY HEIRESS	VAGABOND VIRGIN
DUBIOUS BRIDEGROOM	CAUTIOUS COQUETTE

* Quoted from GOLDEN MULTITUDES: THE STORY OF BEST SELLERS IN THE U. S.

"The king of the mystery field," and "the people's choice
for America's greatest living writer" †
is also the author of

WILLIAM MORROW & CO., NEW YORK, PUBLISHERS

† THE CASE OF ERLE STANLEY GARDNER, by Alva Johnston.